THE
HEADLESS DOLL

Mike Ford

Scholastic Inc.

For Corky and Fats

Copyright © 2024 by Mike Ford

All rights reserved. Published by Scholastic Inc., *Publishers since 1920*. SCHOLASTIC and associated logos are trademarks and/or registered trademarks of Scholastic Inc.

The publisher does not have any control over and does not assume any responsibility for author or third-party websites or their content.

No part of this publication may be reproduced, stored in a retrieval system, or transmitted in any form or by any means, electronic, mechanical, photocopying, recording, or otherwise, without written permission of the publisher. For information regarding permission, write to Scholastic Inc., Attention: Permissions Department, 557 Broadway, New York, NY 10012.

This book is a work of fiction. Names, characters, places, and incidents are either the product of the author's imagination or are used fictitiously, and any resemblance to actual persons, living or dead, business establishments, events, or locales is entirely coincidental.

ISBN 978-1-5461-1176-4

10 9 8 7 6 5 4 3 2 1   24 25 26 27 28

Printed in the U.S.A.   40

First printing 2024

Book design by Stephanie Yang

1

"You should look out at the horizon, not down at the water."

Jennifer turned her head to glance at the boy who had joined her at the railing of the ferry. Dressed in faded jeans and a red T-shirt, he had short black hair and dark brown eyes that looked at her with concern.

"It helps if you're feeling seasick," the boy explained.

Jennifer laughed. "I'm not seasick," she said. "I'm looking for seals."

The boy grinned. "Sorry," he said. "I was trying to be helpful. A lot of people get sick on the trip to the island."

"I don't get sick on boats," Jennifer told him. "Well, not

usually. There was one time on a trip to Antarctica, but that was during a bad storm and the waves were huge. *Everybody* was seasick. Even the crew."

"You've been to Antarctica?" the boy asked.

Jennifer nodded. "I've been a lot of places," she told him. "My parents are naturalists. They write articles and books about the environment. My mother is also a photographer, and she takes the pictures to go with whatever they're working on. They travel all over the world, and sometimes I get to go too."

"Is that why you're going to Big Rock?" the boy asked. "Are they writing about it?"

Jennifer sighed. "No," she said glumly. "My parents are in Costa Rica for the summer, working on a book about spiders. They couldn't take me with them this time, so I'm going to Big Rock to stay with my aunt."

"Who's your aunt?" the boy asked.

"Olivia Shedwater," Jennifer said. "Do you know her?"

"Sure," the boy said. "I know everybody on Big Rock. I

mean, there aren't that many of them. Your aunt's lived here a long time. How come you've never been here before?"

"How do you know I haven't?" Jennifer asked.

"Easy," the boy said. "I've been riding this ferry back and forth since I was born. I was literally born *on* it. And I've never seen you before."

"You were born on the ferry?" Jennifer said.

The boy nodded. "My mother went into labor early, and before they could get to the mainland, I decided it was time to come out. I'm Joe, by the way."

"Jennifer. But my friends call me Jen."

"Welcome to Big Rock, Jen."

"So, you live on the island?" Jen asked.

"Not anymore," Joe said. "After the having-a-baby-on-the-ferry thing, my mother insisted on living someplace where she wouldn't have to depend on a boat to get her where she needed to go. We live on the mainland now. But my uncle owns the only restaurant on Big Rock, and I help out there. I also bring mail and packages over from the post office or take them from the island to the mainland to mail if people don't want to make the trip themselves."

Jennifer looked out at the ocean. In the distance, the island stood out against the blue of the sky. "It's not a very imaginative name," she remarked. "Big Rock Island."

"Well, it *is* a rock," Joe said. "And it is big. The settlers who came here couldn't pronounce the Passamaquoddy name for it, which is *Kci-monossapskuk*, so they just called it what it was, I guess."

"Passamaquoddy?" said Jen.

"That's the name of the tribe that lived in this part of Maine," Joe explained. "I mean, we still do live here. But there were a lot more of us then. So, you never answered my question about why you've never been here before."

"You ask a lot of questions," Jen teased.

"That's how you find out about people," said Joe. "I like hearing people's stories. Like my grandmother says, our stories are our history."

"Well, to answer your question, I've only met my aunt

once, when I was about four, and I barely remember it. We live in California, and I guess she doesn't like to travel. My parents are always going somewhere else. That's why my mom thought it would be fun for me to come here this time."

"You came out here all on your own?" Joe asked.

"Sort of," Jen said. She laughed. "My mom checked in about six hundred times since they put me on the plane this morning. At least she won't be doing that once I'm on the island. There's no cell service or internet there, right?"

"Nope," Joe said. "It's like it's caught in a time warp. No cars either. People get around by foot or on golf carts. Not that there are many places to go."

"It sounds kind of boring," Jen said.

"I think that's why the people who live there like it," said Joe. "And sometimes the quietest people have the most interesting stories. Maybe places are the same way."

"Maybe," Jen said. "Are there any other kids our age there?"

"Just Maddie," Joe said. "She lives there with the Toms."

"The Toms?" said Jen.

"Big Tom and Little Tom," Joe said. "They're lobstermen."

"What's Maddie like?"

Joe hesitated a moment. "Maddie is . . . Maddie," he said.

Before Jen could ask what he meant by that, Joe said, "Here we are."

The ferry was approaching a dock that extended out into the ocean from the shore. A woman standing on the dock waved.

"That's Rita," Joe told Jen. "My uncle's girlfriend. She's the island dockmaster. She also works at the restaurant. And she's the one you call if you need anything fixed."

"Sounds like she does pretty much everything," Jen said.

"She does," Joe agreed. "And she makes the best clam chowder in Maine."

As the ferry pulled up alongside the dock, Joe tossed a thick rope to Rita, who caught it and wrapped it around a cleat. The man piloting the ferry cut the engine, and Joe and Jen hopped off the ferry and onto the dock. As Joe was introducing Jen to Rita, a golf cart rolled up to the end of the dock and stopped. A woman got out. Her red hair was in a thick braid that hung over one shoulder, and the overalls she wore were spattered with paint in every imaginable color. Jen recognized her immediately, mostly because she looked almost exactly like Jen's mother.

"Jen!" Aunt Olivia called out, waving.

Jen waved back. When her aunt reached her, she held out her arms and gave Jen a welcoming hug. "I'm so sorry I wasn't at the mainland to meet your bus from the airport," she said. "I was restringing a doll and lost track of time."

"It's okay, Aunt Olivia," Jen assured her. "I figured it out."

"Oh, call me Liv," her aunt said. "Everybody does. Hi, Rita. Hi, Joe. You got any mail for me?"

"Sure do," Joe said. "And a couple of packages."

"That will be more dolls," Liv said to Jen. "I can't keep up."

Jen knew that her aunt made dolls. They had a couple

of them in their house. But they weren't ordinary dolls. They were what Jen's mother called "art dolls," meaning they weren't meant to be played with; they were meant to be looked at. Aunt Liv's dolls were, well, a little strange. Beautiful, but odd. They felt like they were characters out of fairy tales or maybe dreams. They were mostly human, for example, but some of them had deer antlers or fox tails. Liv sculpted and painted all the faces and made all the clothes they wore herself.

In addition to making the dolls, she also ran a business repairing dolls for other people. She was apparently really good at it, because Jen's mother said people from all over the world sent Liv dolls to be restored or repaired. She referred to the business as a doll hospital, which Jen thought was both funny and a little creepy. She imagined rows and rows of little beds, each one containing a doll that was there to recover.

Joe went back to the ferry and returned with some mail and three large boxes. "Want me to put them in the cart?" he asked.

"Please," Liv said.

She, Jen, and Joe walked to the end of the dock. Joe put the packages in the back of the golf cart, and Jen added her bag to the pile. Then she and Liv got in.

"See you around," Joe said to Jen. "Come to my uncle's. I'm usually there."

"I will," Jen promised.

"You've grown a lot," Liv remarked as she pulled away and navigated the golf cart along a dirt road.

"I was four the last time you saw me," Jen reminded her. "I'm twelve now."

"Really?" her aunt said. "That means I must be—oh dear. Well, let's not think about that. The important thing is that you're here and we're going to have a great summer, right?"

"I hope so," Jen said.

"I know the island feels really remote," Liv said. "I mean, it *is* remote. But it's beautiful here, and you can help me with the dolls."

"Sure," Jen said, although she wasn't convinced dolls were anything to be excited about when she *could* be exploring Costa Rica.

They drove through a group of buildings, and Liv pointed to one of them. "That's Soco's," she said. "Joe's uncle's diner. And that's the little general store. There are a couple of B and Bs for people who come here in the summer to fish. That's how most year-round residents make a living, catering to tourists."

They passed the last house and the road turned and went up a hill. At the top it split into two directions. Liv took the left-hand path. "The other direction heads to the lighthouse," she said. "This one takes us home."

They made one more turn and Liv brought the cart to a stop in front of a huge house. It was much larger than the houses they'd seen earlier. Jen counted three floors. The paint was faded to a pale blue, and there was a screened-in porch that wrapped around the front and sides. All along the edge of the porch there were thick clumps of daisies, their white-and-yellow heads bobbing in the breeze.

"This is it," Liv said as she got out of the golf cart. "Welcome to Pratchett House."

"Pratchett?" said Jen.

"That was the name of the man who built it," Liv explained. "Well, he *had* it built for him. People on the island mostly call it the dollhouse." She laughed as she took the boxes from the back of the cart. "You can guess why."

Jen got her bag and followed her aunt up the steps to the porch. There was a small black cat sitting beside the door. It looked at Jen with pale green eyes.

"That's Nix," Liv said as she opened the door.

"Hey, Nix," said Jen, bending and rubbing the cat's head.

Jen walked into the house while Nix trotted down the steps and into the yard. Inside, Pratchett House was a little cooler than it was outside, but not by much.

"There's no air-conditioning," Liv explained. "But it

cools down at night, and there's almost always a nice breeze coming in from the sea."

Jen looked around at the big room they were standing in. The ceilings were high, the floors were beautiful dark wood, and the walls were covered in wallpaper with a fancy design of flowers and birds.

"Wow," Jen said. "It looks like an old-fashioned hotel."

Her aunt laughed. "You sound like Chester McKiser."

"Who?"

"Chester owns the lighthouse on the island," Liv explained. "He's been after me for years to sell him this house so he can turn it into a hotel. He thinks it would be the perfect tourist destination. And he's probably right. At least half the people here agree with him."

"What about the other half?" Jen asked.

"We like the island the way it is," Liv said. "Quiet. We don't want it overrun with tourists."

Jen, looking around, noticed a black cat curled up on top of a bookcase, sleeping. "Didn't I just see you outside?" she said.

12

"That's the other Nix," her aunt said. "Well, one of them."

"How many are there?" Jen asked.

"Six," Liv answered. "No, seven. Maybe eight." She sighed. "I don't really know. They all look the same and they're never all in one place at one time."

"And they're all named Nix?"

"It makes it easier," said Liv. "Come on, I'll show you the rest of the house."

After a quick tour of the first floor, which included the kitchen and three other rooms like the first one, they went upstairs to the second floor.

"This is where my workroom is," Liv told Jen as they walked down a hallway lined with doors. "And most of the other rooms are filled with doll stuff too. I'm afraid it's all kind of a mess. The bedrooms are on the third floor."

They went up another flight of stairs and into another hallway with more doors. "My bedroom is here," Liv said, indicating one of the doors. "And I thought you might like the Yellow Room. It's on a corner and gets lots of light and nice breezes."

She went to the end of the hall and into a room. When Jen entered, she saw immediately why it was called the Yellow Room. The walls were covered in wallpaper patterned with yellow roses, and the curtains at the window were a buttery yellow. The quilt on the bed was pieced together out of different shades of yellow, and on the dresser was a yellow vase holding a bouquet of daisies.

"You've got your own bathroom," Liv said, pointing to a door.

Jen poked her head into the bathroom, which, unsurprisingly, was tiled in yellow and had yellow towels hanging from the bar beside the sink.

"It's cute," she said.

"Why don't you unpack while I make us some dinner," Liv suggested. "Do you like spaghetti?"

"I love it," Jen said.

Her aunt left, and Jen set her bag on the bed and opened

it. As she took her things out, she thought that maybe a summer on Big Rock Island might not be so bad after all. She'd already made one friend. And although she hadn't spent much time with Aunt Liv, she had a feeling they were going to get along really well.

She carried a stack of T-shirts to the dresser and pulled the top drawer open. She was about to set the shirts inside when she saw that there was already something in there.

It was an eye.

Jen hesitated a moment, then reached in and picked the eye up. It was made of glass, which was a relief, but it looked real. She held it up. The iris was blue, with flecks of brown and gold. It was so realistic that Jen wouldn't have been at all surprised if it had blinked at her.

Jen slipped the eye into her pocket and put the T-shirts in the drawer. She shut it and went back to the bed. For some reason, finding the eye made her feel like she was being watched. She knew it was silly to think such a thing, but she could feel the eye in her pocket, and it made her wonder how it had gotten into the drawer. It was almost as if someone had left it in there to scare her.

Suddenly, she didn't want to be alone in the Yellow Room. It felt creepy.

She left her bag half-unpacked and hurried down the hall to the stairs.

2

"I wondered where that got to."

Aunt Liv took the eye that Jen held out to her. She glanced at the cat lying in a puddle of sunshine on the kitchen floor. "Did one of you take this?"

The cat looked up, yawned, then rolled over onto its other side.

"The Nixes are always taking things," Liv told Jen. "The problem is finding where they *put* them."

Jen couldn't imagine how a cat might have opened the dresser drawer, dropped the eye inside, and closed it again, but she supposed it might be possible. "It looks so real," she said. "It kind of freaked me out."

"Sorry," Liv said. "That's one of the things my customers love about them. It took me a long time to figure out how to make them so realistic."

"You made that?" Jen said.

"I did," said Liv. "This particular eye belongs to a doll named Claudia. I'll introduce you to her later if you want."

Jen wasn't sure she did want that, but she nodded anyway. "What can I do to help with dinner?" she asked.

"You can get some plates and silverware," Liv said. "Plates are in the cupboard next to the sink. Silverware is in the top drawer."

Jen went to the cupboard and opened it. Inside was a stack of plates, not one of them the same pattern or color. She took the two topmost ones and set them on the table. Then she opened the silverware drawer. It was a jumble of forks, spoons, and knives. Again, none of them matched, so she picked two forks she liked and set them beside the plates.

"The sauce should be hot enough," Liv said as she took

the spaghetti pot to the sink and emptied the contents into a waiting colander. "We can dish it up right from the stove. Saves time when it comes to washing up."

A minute or two later, they were seated at the table. Jen stuck her fork into the tangle of noodles on her plate, twirled it, and popped it into her mouth. The bright taste of tomatoes and herbs burst over her tongue.

"This is fantastic," she told her aunt.

"You like it?" she said. "Everything in it came from my garden. I make a bunch of sauce every summer. It's especially nice in the winter. Reminds me that it won't always be cold. The green beans are also from the garden."

"Did you make the bread too?" Jen asked, taking a bite of the thick chunk she'd broken off from a loaf that was on the table.

"That I did not make," Liv said. "Alex did. Alex Socobasin. Joe's uncle. He's a fantastic baker."

"I wish we had a garden," Jen said. "Back home, I mean. But Mom and Dad travel so much and are always busy with deadlines. Mom spends most of her time working on her photography."

"That sounds like Steph," Olivia said. "When we were about your age, she found an old camera at a yard sale. The kind that uses film. She got really into learning how to use it. She and our dad even built a darkroom in our basement so she could develop the film herself. Steph spent hours down there. And she got good at it."

"She still uses that camera sometimes," Jen said. "She says it's good to be reminded of how much harder it used to be to take pictures."

"She's right," Olivia said. "Technology has made a lot of things easier, but when it comes to art, I prefer doing things by hand. It's why people like my dolls. They like knowing I made everything myself."

"How did you get interested in dolls?" Jen asked her. "Did you find one at a yard sale?"

Her aunt laughed. "Not quite," she said. "I saw a puppet show. Marionettes, actually. It was at a Renaissance festival.

They were telling the story of Beauty and the Beast. And I was fascinated by the puppets. How the costumes looked. How they moved. How *real* they felt. I wanted to make things like that. I found a doll-making class and started there. Then I found people who were doing the sorts of things I wanted to do, and I begged them to teach me. It kind of grew from there."

"Wow," Jen said. "You and Mom both found things you love to do. I wish I had something like that."

"You don't have anything you love doing?" Liv asked.

Jen shrugged. "I'm interested in a lot of things," she said. "But I'm not great at any one thing in particular."

"You'll find your thing," Liv assured her. "It's waiting for you to find it. And there's no rush."

"That's what Mom says too," said Jen. "I just wish I had *some* idea. I change my mind every other week."

"You know what might help you decide?" Liv said.

"What?" said Jen.

"A piece of cake."

Liv got up and went to the refrigerator. When she came

back, she was carrying two small plates, each holding a slice of cake.

"Lemon-blueberry shortcake," she said, setting a plate in front of Jen. "Also made by Alex."

Jen forked a piece of cake into her mouth. It was delicious. She quickly took a second bite, then a third. Soon, there were only crumbs left on her plate.

"I think that's the best cake I've ever had," she said.

"Made with blueberries picked right here on the island," Liv said. "So, you ready to meet Claudia?"

"I'm not sure," Jen said. "A one-eyed doll sounds a little creepy."

"She won't have one eye for long," said Liv. "Now that you found her other one, I can finish repairing her. Come on. She won't bite. I promise."

They went into the living room. But instead of heading for the stairs, Liv opened a door that Jen had thought was a closet. It revealed a set of stairs going down to the cellar.

"I thought your workroom was upstairs," Jen said.

22

"It is," Liv answered. "But all the electric woodworking tools are downstairs."

She turned a light on and went down the stairs, with Jen right behind her.

"I'm building a display stand for Claudia, so she's down here," Liv explained.

The basement was not the damp, musty place Jen had expected. It had a stone floor that was covered in sawdust. One wall had rows of shelves that held jars of vegetables and sauces. Workbenches lined two of the other walls. And at the far end there was a door that Jen guessed led to the outside.

"Here she is," Liv said, going over to one of the workbenches, where a large doll stood. "Jen, meet Claudia."

Jen went over and looked at the doll. She was about two feet tall. Her hair was long and black, and her head was ceramic. She was missing an eye, but the other one perfectly matched the one Jen had found in the dresser drawer. Claudia's body was made out of cloth, but her hands and feet were also ceramic.

23

"I haven't finished her dress yet," Liv said. "It has a lot of hand embroidery on it, so it's taking a long time. It's going to be beautiful when it's done."

"She looks like she's old," Jen remarked.

"She is," Liv said. "And very valuable. She should probably be in a museum, but her mother would never part with her."

"Her mother?" said Jen.

"The woman she belongs to," Liv explained. "I know it sounds a little strange. A lot of doll collectors don't think of the dolls as simply things they own. They have very strong connections to them. Almost like they are their children."

Jen thought that made sense, even if it was maybe kind of weird. She wondered what Claudia's mother was like. She had never been into dolls herself, even when she was younger, so she didn't understand the appeal of collecting them. In fact, she thought dolls were a little bit creepy, like miniature people but not alive.

There were half a dozen other dolls on the workbenches,

in various stages of repair. She guessed these were ones that were waiting for stands to be made, or maybe even body parts, since a couple were made out of wood.

"Want to take a little walk around the island?" Liv asked. "It'll be light for a while yet."

Jen, more than happy to get out of the basement filled with dolls, nodded. "That sounds great."

Instead of going back upstairs, Liv walked to the door at the end of the room. "This leads out into the back garden," she said as she opened it.

They stepped out into a riot of color. The yard behind the house was filled with all kinds of flowers. In addition, there was a big vegetable garden featuring orderly rows of greens.

"It's early in the year, but we have a lot of lettuces, asparagus, beans, peas, and some eggplant," Liv said as she walked Jen through the garden. "Tomatoes are coming along nicely too. And, of course, all the herbs. By the time summer is over, you'll probably be tired of basil and tomato sandwiches."

"Not if they're on that bread we had at dinner," Jen assured her. "It will be fun to pick everything."

"I hope you feel that way after a few weeks of weeding," Liv said. "But yeah, things you've grown yourself always taste better."

They continued around to the front of the house, then along the road they'd driven up earlier. This time when they reached the split, they took the left-hand path. It went on for a little way, then made a sharp turn. When they rounded it, Jen saw the lighthouse.

Unlike most lighthouses she'd seen, this one wasn't round. It had four sides, and it was made out of stone blocks. At the top, a walkway went all around the part that held the light, with only a narrow railing to hold on to. Beside the lighthouse was a small cottage covered in cedar shingles.

"Does someone live here?" Jen asked.

"Not at the moment," Liv said. "Chester McKiser, the man I told you about, wants to tear it down and build a bigger house here. But the lighthouse is a historic landmark, so he has to get special permission to do that, and some of us have objected."

"I bet he doesn't like that," Jen said.

"No, he doesn't," her aunt said. She sounded a little angry.

"Can we go inside the lighthouse?" Jen asked.

"I'm afraid not," Liv said. "It's locked to prevent anyone from going up it and getting hurt. But we can look at the view."

She walked around the side of the lighthouse. Behind it, the ground stopped about thirty feet away from the light-house, dropping off at a cliff. Beyond that was the sea, green and gray and seemingly endless. Jen and Liv stood back from the edge and looked out at it. Herring gulls and terns wheeled in the sky, screeching and sometimes dipping down to the water before rising back up again.

"Is that a puffin?" Jen asked, catching sight of a bird with a distinctive orange beak.

"Good eye," said Liv. "We have a small colony of them that nest on the island. They're one of the attractions. Birders come out here to see them."

"I read up on the local wildlife," Jen told her. "I like to do that wherever we go."

"You don't want to get too close to that edge," a voice said. "Wind picks up, it could toss you right over."

Jen turned around. Standing beside the lighthouse was a man. Jen couldn't help but notice that when her aunt saw him, she frowned.

"Chester," she said.

"Olivia," the man said. He looked at Jen. "And who might this be?"

"My niece," Liv said. "Jennifer. She's staying with me for the summer."

"That so?" said Chester. "Well, make sure she doesn't come around my property unattended. Wouldn't want anything to happen to her."

"No," Liv said. "We wouldn't."

"You give any more thought to selling that house?" Chester asked.

"Not since the last time you asked, Chester," said Liv. "And the answer is still no."

"Let me know when you change your mind," Chester said. "Course, the price I'm willing to pay goes down the longer you wait, so don't take too long."

"I'm not going to sell, Chester," said Liv as she started walking away. "Ever."

Jen followed her aunt.

"Nice to meet you, Jenny," Chester said as she walked by.

Jen nodded but didn't say anything until they were far enough away that Chester couldn't hear them. "I hate being called Jenny," she said.

Her aunt laughed. "Don't pay any attention to Chester," she said. "He doesn't like it when he doesn't get what he wants. And he's never getting my house."

"Good," Jen said. She hadn't even spent one night in the house, but she felt protective of it.

"Sometimes I wish Arthur would take care of Chester," Liv said.

"Who's Arthur?"

"A ghost," said Liv. "Well, he wasn't always a ghost. Arthur Crunk was the lighthouse keeper a very long time ago. Local legend says his ghost still haunts the lighthouse."

A cold breeze, like invisible breath, blew across Jen's skin, making her shiver. "Have you ever seen him?"

"It's just a story," her aunt said.

That wasn't really an answer. Jen wanted to ask more about the ghost of Arthur Crunk. Then she thought about the eye in her dresser, and about how she'd felt like someone—or something—was watching her. Maybe that was enough weird stuff for her first day.

"We can explore the island more tomorrow," Liv said. "Let's go home. I think there might be two pieces of cake left."

That sounded like the best idea Jen had heard all day.

3

"Good morning."

Liv looked up at Jen from where she was seated at the table, writing something on a piece of paper. "Morning," she said cheerfully. "How'd you sleep?"

"Pretty well," Jen answered. "The thunder woke me up a couple of times."

"Thunder?" Liv said.

Jen nodded. "It sounded like it was right over the house." She glanced out one of the windows. Outside, it was sunny and clear. "It doesn't look like it rained, though. That's weird."

"It didn't," Liv said. "There was no storm last night. Maybe you dreamed it?"

"Maybe," Jen said. "But it sounded so real."

"First night in a new house," her aunt said, as if this explained everything. "Do you drink tea? I made some. Mint. Or there's orange juice in the fridge. I thought we'd go to Soco's for breakfast. You can meet Alex."

"Tea sounds great," Jen said. "And so does breakfast."

"Mugs are in the cupboard that Nix is sitting beneath," Liv said.

Jen went over to the cat, who was perched on the counter, and rubbed its ears. Nix mewed and gently patted her hand with a paw. Jen got a mug from the cupboard, then poured tea from a ceramic teapot shaped like a fish. The tea burbled from its lips, the scent of mint rising up.

"There's cream and sugar over here," Liv said.

Jen sat down at the table, added a little sugar to the tea, and sipped it. She watched as her aunt wrote something down on the paper in front of her. Liv sighed.

"I'm making a to-do list," she said. "Doll stuff. There's so much to get done."

"Can I help?" Jen asked.

"Actually, you can," said Liv. "I really need to pack up some orders and get them to the mainland to mail. How about later on I show you how to do that?"

"Sounds fun," said Jen.

"It's not," said Liv, laughing. "Unless you're really into boxes and packing materials and tape. But speaking of dolls, I don't suppose you went down to the cellar last night to look at them, did you? It's okay if you did."

Jen shook her head. She didn't want to tell Liv that going into a cellar to look at dolls in the middle of the night was one of the *last* things she wanted to do. "No," she said. "Why?"

"Claudia was lying on the workbench," Liv said. "It's not a big deal. I probably didn't secure her to the stand properly. Or maybe a Nix got down there somehow. She's fine. But if she'd fallen on the floor, she might have gotten broken."

"Maybe she wakes up at night," Jen said. "I read a book like that once, about a dollhouse where the dolls inside came to life every night and got into all kinds of trouble."

"I can't even imagine what kind of mischief *my* dolls would get into," Liv said. "Especially some of the more unusual ones."

Jen thought about this as she finished her tea. She'd read the book about the dollhouse when she was eight or nine and had mostly forgotten about it until now. But at the time it had given her nightmares. For weeks she dreamed about being trapped inside a dollhouse, looking out the tiny windows and seeing what appeared to be a giant eye staring back at her. The eye belonged to the girl whose bedroom the dollhouse was in. She wasn't a giant at all, but in the dream, Jen had shrunk to the size of a tiny dollhouse figure, so everything outside the dollhouse looked huge.

No wonder finding that eye freaked you out, she thought.

When she was done with her tea, she rinsed the mug in the sink. Then she and her aunt left to, as Liv put it, "go into town," even though it was really just a short walk and the small group of houses and other buildings was barely a village, let alone a town. Ten minutes after they left the house, they walked into Soco's. The restaurant had half a dozen tables, plus a counter lined with stools. The place was empty except for a man standing behind the counter.

"Morning, Alex," Liv said as she took a seat at the counter.

"Hey, Liv," the man said. Then he looked at Jen. "And you must be the mysterious stranger my nephew told me about."

"Jen," said Jen. "And I don't know about mysterious."

"How about hungry?" Alex asked.

"That I definitely am," said Jen.

"I know what your aunt will have," said Alex. "Blueberry pancakes, right?"

"Yep," said Liv. "Been thinking about them since I woke up."

"Pancakes sound great," Jen said. "I'll have those too."

"Two stacks of blueberry pancakes coming right up," Alex said. He went to a stove and began cooking, but also continued talking to them. "What do you think of the dollhouse, Jen?" he asked.

"It's interesting," Jen said.

Alex laughed. "You mean creepy," he said.

"Hey!" Liv exclaimed. "It's not creepy."

Alex pointed a spatula at her. "Not the house, no," he said. "It's all those dolls running around in it."

"They're not running," said Liv. "They're mostly standing. Or lying down. Or sitting. Definitely not running."

"I'm not so sure about that," Alex teased as he flipped over the pancakes on the griddle. "I think at night they have parties. I bet they sneak into your room and watch you sleep. Jen, you should probably listen for the sound of little footsteps on the stairs." He tapped on the wooden countertop with the end of the spatula, mimicking the sound of someone walking.

Jen laughed, but part of her was also creeped out by the

thought of a doll making its way upstairs and down the hall to her room. Again, she thought about the book that had scared her so much when she was younger.

"The only little feet on the stairs belong to the Nixes," Liv said.

Alex came over, carrying two plates stacked with pancakes. "That you *know* of," he said as he set them down in front of Jen and her aunt.

Jen poured some syrup on her pancakes from a bottle on the counter, then took a bite.

"What do you think?" Alex asked.

"Delishusss," Jen said, her mouth still full.

"Another satisfied customer," said Alex. "I'll make you some more."

He went back to the stove while Jen devoured the rest of her pancakes. By the time she was done, Alex arrived and added two more to her plate.

When she finished those, Jen set her fork down. "Those were the best pancakes I've ever had," she told Alex.

"Come back anytime for more," he said. "What are you two going to do next?"

"I have some work I need to get done on a rush order," Liv said. "Jen, do you want to explore the island on your own for a while? You can't really get lost. The road circles the island and ends at the dock. You know how to get home from there."

"That sounds fun," said Jen. "Then this afternoon you can show me how to pack the dolls up for mailing."

"If you run into any of those dolls while you're walking around the island, don't talk to them," Alex said seriously. "I hear sometimes one gets loose. Supposedly, there's a group of them that live in the forest."

Liv groaned. "Bye, Alex," she said. "We'll see you later."

Jen waved at Alex, who grinned. Then she and her aunt left the diner.

"Okay, you know where the house is," Liv said. "And like I said, you can't get lost. Just be careful going on rocks or anything like that. They can be slippery."

"Got it," Jen said. "No slippery rocks. I'll see you back at the house."

Liv started walking back up the hill toward home while Jen took the opposite direction. She passed through the village, then kept going. The road ran along the edge of the island, and the farther she walked, the fewer houses there were. The ones nearest the ocean often had docks, with small boats tied up at them. Jen wondered what it would be like to live so close to the water, to be able to see it right outside the windows.

She came to a place where the road ran alongside a beach. Stepping off the road and onto the sand, she took off her sneakers and walked to the edge of the water. The sea was calm, and the waves that landed on the shore were small and gentle. They raced up the beach and covered her toes in cold, clear water.

Jen walked along, looking at the birds that floated on the surface of the ocean. Then, ahead of her, she saw a single huge rock resting half in the sand and half in the water. The top of the rock was flat, and someone was sitting cross-legged on it. Whoever it was wore a red hoodie with the top covering their head, so Jen had no idea what the person looked like. They were holding a book in their hands, reading.

When Jen got closer, she stopped and looked up at the person on the rock. Now she saw that it was a girl. And the book she was reading was *The Shining*, by Stephen King.

"Your name isn't Maddie, is it?" Jen asked.

The girl barely glanced at her. "Who wants to know?" she said curtly.

"I'm Jen. Joe told me there was a girl on the island named Maddie. I thought that might be you."

The girl lowered her book and gave Jen a longer stare. "Yeah, that's me," she said. "What do you want?"

"Nothing," Jen said. She didn't know why Maddie sounded so angry. "I just wanted to say hi. I'm staying here for the summer."

"So?" Maddie said.

Jen wasn't sure how to answer this. "I thought it would be nice to have a friend," she said after a moment. "Since there aren't any other kids here."

"I don't do friends," Maddie said, and she lifted her book up so that it was covering her face.

Jen started to say something, then changed her mind. If Maddie didn't want to be friendly, that was her problem, not Jen's. She was disappointed that the only other girl her age on the island had no interest in even trying to get to know her, but there was nothing she could do about that.

"Guess I'll see you around," she said, and walked away.

Part of her hoped that Maddie would tell her to stop, maybe call her back and apologize for being rude. But that didn't happen. Jen suspected that if she turned around, Maddie would still be sitting on top of the rock, reading, not caring at all that Jen was leaving. In fact, she was probably happy that Jen was leaving.

At least there's Joe, she thought. But Joe didn't live on the island. He was only there sometimes. It would have been nice to have someone else to hang out with.

The waves continued to wash over Jen's feet. But now her mood had changed, and it was no longer fun. The water felt cold, and the sand between her toes was kind of scratchy. Even the little crab that darted over and poked her with one tiny claw before scuttling away again didn't make her laugh. Jen decided maybe it was time to head back to the house.

Unfortunately, she also realized that the beach had come to an end, and there was no way to get back on the road from where she was, as here it went up a low hill that was too steep to climb from the beach. She had to walk back past the rock Maddie was sitting on. At least, she thought, she could walk behind it. Maybe Maddie wouldn't even notice her. Probably, she wouldn't. And what did it matter if she did?

Jen tried not to think about it as she made her way back to the other end of the beach. She didn't even look at Maddie as she passed behind the rock. But when she was a few feet on the other side, she heard Maddie say, "The ghosts don't like strangers."

Jen stopped. She turned around. "What ghosts?"

Maddie was still reading her book. "The ones on the island," she said. "There are lots of ghosts here. And they don't like strangers. I thought you should know."

Jen had no idea what the girl was talking about. "Thanks for the warning," she said, and turned away to continue her walk.

Again, she waited for Maddie to say something else. Something that made sense. But apparently, she'd said all she had to say, because Jen walked the rest of the way down the beach without hearing another word. When she reached the road again, she took one quick look behind her. In the distance, Maddie's red hoodie stood out against the darkness of the rock.

"Ghosts," Jen muttered. "Living dolls and ghosts. What's next, vampires? Maybe a werewolf?"

Big Rock Island was turning out to be weirder than she

could have imagined. And Maddie was a big disappointment. At least Aunt Liv was great. And Alex and Joe. They
made up for people like Chester McKiser and now Maddie.
Still, Maddie's reaction to her made her feel bad.

She took a deep breath, trying to push the feeling out of
her mind. She closed her eyes and felt the sun warm her
face. She listened to the sound of birds, and the gentle mur-
muring of the sea. These things made her feel better.

"Boo!"

Jen gave a little shriek and opened her eyes.

Maddie walked by her.

"I told you, watch out for the ghosts," she said, and
laughed.

Jen watched her walk away. "I think maybe it's you I
need to watch out for, not ghosts," she muttered to herself.

Then she began the long walk back to the house.

4

"You're back earlier than I expected," Aunt Liv said when Jen walked into her workroom.

"Yeah," Jen said.

Her aunt set down the doll she was working on. "Everything okay?"

Jen shrugged. She didn't want to admit that she wasn't feeling all that great about the rest of the summer. "I ran into Maddie," she said.

"Ran into," Liv repeated. "Sounds like you were in a car accident. I take it she was her usual friendly self?"

"Is she always like that?" Jen asked.

"No," Liv answered. "Not always. But a lot of the time. Don't take it personally. I think she's in a difficult phase. Unfortunately, she's been in it for six or seven years."

Jen sighed. "It was like she'd decided I was a horrible person before she even knew who I was."

"Give her time to get to know you," said Liv.

"I don't think she wants to get to know me," Jen said. "At least there's Joe."

"Speaking of Joe, let me show you how to box up the dolls," Liv said. "We can get a couple done for the ferry ride to the mainland this afternoon."

She led Jen out of the workroom and into the next room. This one had cardboard boxes piled up in it, and there was a big table covered with stacks of newspaper, rolls of tape, brown wrapping paper, and black markers. Six dolls of various sizes stood on a bench against one of the walls.

"These are ready to travel back to their homes," Liv said. "We have to pack them carefully to make sure they get there safely."

For the next little while she showed Jen how to prepare a box for a doll, first cocooning it in several layers of newspapers and then laying it in a nest of shredded packing material. Then she sealed the box with tape and wrapped the box in brown paper. Finally, she wrote the address the doll was going to on the package.

"You do the next one," Liv said. She indicated a piece of paper on the table. "The address is the next one on the list."

She supervised while Jen boxed up one of the dolls. "Perfect," she said when the box was wrapped and labeled. "I'm going to leave you to do the rest. Then we can take them down to the dock and give them to Joe."

Left alone to finish the job, Jen focused her attention on making sure the dolls were packed up correctly. But pretty soon she found herself thinking about her encounter with Maddie. Why did the other girl have to be so mean? If Jen was the only kid living on an island, she'd be thrilled to meet someone her own age. But Maddie had treated her like she was an unwanted nuisance.

She was pretty sure Aunt Liv was wrong about Maddie getting to know her. How could she get to know her when she'd told Jen she "didn't do friends"? Given her bad attitude, Jen hoped she wouldn't see much of Maddie at all.

Then she thought about what Maddie had told her about watching out for ghosts. What was *that* supposed to mean? Was she just trying to scare Jen? Did she really believe there was such a thing as ghosts? Given the kinds of books she liked to read, maybe she did.

Aunt Liv had mentioned a ghost too. The one who supposedly haunted the lighthouse. Maybe it was an island thing, believing in them. Like something they made up for tourists. Jen knew from her travels with her parents that people loved to believe all kinds of wild things about the places they visited. Once, in New Orleans, the three of them had even gone on a ghost tour of the supposedly haunted places in the city. There were a *lot* of them, and the woman leading the group had all kinds of gruesome stories to tell about ghosts that wanted revenge, ghosts that were still searching for their lost loves, and ghosts that appeared to give warnings, but after walking around for hours they hadn't seen a single one.

"How's it going?"

Aunt Liv's question brought Jen back to the moment.

"Great," she said. "All done."

"Wow," Liv said, inspecting the packages. "I can't tell you what a help it is having someone to do this part of the business."

"I like wrapping," Jen told her. "You should see me at Christmas. Dad says I should go to work for Santa."

Her aunt laughed. "Not if I hire you first," she said. "Let's take these down to the dock. The ferry will be coming in soon."

They took the packages out to the golf cart. "You want to drive?" Liv asked as she got into the passenger seat.

"Really?" Jen said.

"It's easy," Liv said. "I'll walk you through it."

After a couple of jerky starts, Jen found herself steering

the cart along the road to town. They got to the dock just as Joe and Rita were unloading boxes from the ferry. Alex was also there, as some of the boxes were supplies for the diner.

"Hey," he said sternly. "I'm going to need to see your license."

"She picked it up right away," Aunt Liv said. "She'll be ready for the Big Rock Grand Prix in no time."

"The what?" Jen asked.

"The annual golf cart race around the island," Joe explained. "We do three laps. Whoever wins gets to keep the trophy for the next year. It sat in the diner for four years, and I want it back."

"Who has it now?"

"Maddie," said Joe. "She's won two years in a row. She'll run you right off the road if you're not careful. She gets that from her uncle."

"Is her uncle a race car driver?" Jen asked.

Joe snorted. "Chester? No. He'll just do anything to win."

"You mean Chester McKiser?" said Jen. "He's Maddie's uncle?"

Joe nodded. "You've heard of him?"

"I've met him," Jen said. "Last night."

As she helped load the boxes of dolls onto the ferry, she thought about the two recent encounters she'd had. Now that she knew Maddie and Chester were related, it made sense. They were a lot alike.

"Joe, I'm going to get a cup of coffee and some of Soco's blueberry pie before we head to the other side," the ferry captain said once the boxes were on board. "Be back in about half an hour, okay?"

Joe nodded. "Want to go explore in the woods?" he asked Jen. "I can show you where some foxes live."

Jen looked at her aunt. "Is that okay?"

"Sure," Liv said. "See you later."

Joe and Jen walked to the edge of the forest, then stepped into the trees. Jen couldn't see a path, but Joe seemed to know exactly where they were going. As they passed the different trees, he touched them lightly with his fingertips. "White spruce," he said. "Paper birch. Balsam fir." He noticed Jen watching him and looked a little embarrassed. "Sorry. I just like to say their names."

"Don't be sorry," said Jen. "I think it's great. I don't know much about trees."

"I love the forest," Joe said. "Red maple. Yellow birch. I spend a lot of time in here."

"You said there are foxes?" Jen asked.

Joe nodded. "We should stop talking, so we don't scare them off."

They continued on, going up a slope. At the top, Joe stopped and squatted. Jen did the same. Joe pointed ahead of them. Jen looked. At first, she didn't see anything. Then she noticed some rustling in a clump of ferns. A moment later, a fox kit emerged, followed by a second. The two little foxes sniffed around in the moss. Then one of them pounced on the other, and they started rolling around in a tangle of tails and paws.

Jen couldn't help but laugh. The foxes stopped playing and looked in their direction, their ears pointed up. Then they dashed back into the ferns.

"Whoops," Jen said. "But they were really cute."

"They're about to start learning how to hunt with their parents," Joe told her. "I love foxes."

"I have a feeling you love *all* animals," Jen said. "And trees."

Joe laughed. "Pretty much anything in the outdoors," he said. Then he smacked at something on his upper arm. "Except blackflies. They bite."

They stood and continued walking through the woods, heading back the way they'd come.

"I met Maddie," Jen told Joe.

"It had to happen sometime," Joe said. "How'd it go?"

"She told me I should watch out for ghosts," said Jen. "She said they don't like strangers."

"That sounds like Maddie," said Joe. "Don't pay any attention to her."

"My aunt mentioned a ghost too," Jen said. "At the lighthouse."

"Arthur," said Joe as if they were talking about just another resident of the island.

"What's that about?"

"Arthur was the lighthouse keeper," Joe said. "You probably know that part."

Jen nodded. "But why does he supposedly haunt it?"

"He was responsible for a bad shipwreck," Joe told her. "He was drunk and forgot to light the light during a storm. A trading ship returning from England crashed onto the rocks offshore and sank. Everybody drowned."

"That's terrible," Jen said.

"It gets worse," said Joe. "The captain lived on the island. He had a little girl named Pearl. Pearl went down to the beach, hoping to find her father alive. She didn't. But she did find a doll he had brought back for her from his trip. It had washed ashore. It was broken, and the head was missing. Pearl sat on the beach cradling it and caught a chill that turned into a fever. She died a few days later, still holding that doll in her arms."

"So, Arthur haunts the lighthouse because he feels guilty about not lighting the light," said Jen.

"And particularly about the death of Pearl Pratchett," Joe said. "I guess he was very close to her and she used to help him around the lighthouse."

"Wait," said Jen. "Did you say Pratchett?"

"Yeah," Joe said. "Captain Pratchett and Pearl Pratchett."

"And I'm guessing they lived in Pratchett House?" said Jen. "As in the house my aunt lives in now?"

"Oh," Joe said. "Yeah. I forgot that's its name. We all call it the dollhouse."

Jen was regretting that she had asked about ghosts. She still didn't believe in them, but the story about the shipwreck and Pearl Pratchett's death was really sad. If ghosts were real, she could understand why Arthur Crunk might still be hanging around the lighthouse. He must have been tormented by thinking the shipwreck and all those deaths were his fault.

"You okay?" Joe asked, interrupting Jen's thoughts. "I didn't scare you with that story, did I? It's just that you asked about Arthur."

"No, it's fine," said Jen. She forced a smile. "But how about the rest of the way back you tell me the names of the trees?"

She said goodbye to Joe at the wharf and headed back to Pratchett House. This time as she walked up the steps, she felt a sense of foreboding that she hadn't felt the other times she'd gone into the house. Now that she knew the tragic history of the original inhabitants, it was hard not to.

When she got inside, Aunt Liv was in the kitchen. "Perfect timing," she said. "I just made some mint iced tea. Sit down and tell me all about your walk with Joe."

As Jen sipped at the glass of tea her aunt brought her, she told Liv what Joe had told her about the Pratchetts.

"That's the way I heard the story too," said Aunt Liv. "Sad, isn't it? And Pearl's mother died giving birth to her, so the whole story is a tragedy."

"Poor Pearl," Jen said. "Never knew her mother. Then her father drowned. I don't think she died from a fever. I think she died from a broken heart."

"There's a portrait of her in the Pink Room," Liv told her. "Want to see it?"

Jen hesitated. Pearl's story was so sad. But her curiosity got the better of her, and she nodded.

They went up to the third floor, where Aunt Liv opened the door to a room Jen hadn't yet been in. True to its name, it was painted pink, and almost everything in it was some shade of that color.

"Was this her room?" Jen asked.

"Yes," Liv said. "Pink was apparently her favorite color." She sighed. "She died right here."

Pearl's portrait hung on a wall all by itself. It was enclosed in a dark wood frame. The image showed a young girl with blue eyes and blonde hair in curls that fell past her shoulders. She was wearing a fancy blue dress. In her arms she held a doll that looked a lot like her.

"Do you think that's the doll her father was bringing back for her?" Jen said.

"Maybe a likeness of it," Liv said. "Or at least what the portrait painter thought it looked like. Supposedly the head was missing when Pearl found it on the beach."

"Joe mentioned that too," said Jen.

"The painting is dated 1825," Liv told Jen. "It was done the year after Pearl died, by a woman who lived here on the island. The same artist painted a portrait of Captain Pratchett, which is hanging downstairs. I guess she wanted the two of them to still be together in the house, in a way. That one is unusual because it's painted directly onto the wall. I don't know why, but it's very interesting."

Jen looked at Pearl's face. She had a beautiful but sad expression on her face. The doll she held had a similar one on its painted face. Jen searched for a word to describe how they looked. Then it came to her.

Haunted.

Both Pearl and the doll looked haunted.

5

The sound of the storm woke Jen up.

She shivered. The room was colder than it ought to be in summertime. She got out of bed and walked over to the window to shut it. As she started to slide the window down, though, she realized that outside, the night was clear and calm. There was no rain.

She raised the screen and stretched out her hand. The air outside the house was warm. It was only cold *inside* the house. At first, she thought maybe the air-conditioning had gone into overdrive. Then she remembered that there was no air-conditioning.

That's why the windows were open in the first place.

Then why do I hear rain on the roof? she wondered.

As if to taunt her, the sound of thunder laughed overhead.

Jen went to the light switch by the door and flipped it on. Nothing happened. She tried several more times, with the same result. The power was out. The moonlight coming in the window was bright, though, and she could see well enough that she wasn't afraid of bumping into anything. But bumping into things wasn't really what she was afraid of.

The invisible rain began to fall harder.

"You're dreaming," Jen told herself. But she wasn't dreaming. She was wide-awake. She could feel the soft rug beneath her bare feet. She could look out the window into the garden and hear insects chirping in the warm summer night. Yet somehow, there was a storm raging.

"My daddy is over the ocean."

The voice was barely a whisper. It floated through the air like the softest breeze. A girl's voice. She recognized the tune. It was "My Bonnie Lies over the Ocean," a song she'd learned a long time ago in music class at school. Only the words were a little different.

Jen waited to see if the voice would come again. Just when she thought she must have imagined it, it did.

"My daddy is over the sea."

This time it was a little bit louder. But Jen still couldn't tell where it was coming from. It was like hearing a song being played somewhere outside and only being able to catch bits and pieces of it.

This song wasn't coming from outside, though. It was coming from somewhere inside the house.

Jen turned the doorknob and pulled the bedroom door open. The hallway stretched out ahead of her, darker than her room because the moonlight didn't reach much past her doorway.

"My daddy is over the ocean."

The voice was stronger now. It came from the far end of the hall. The end where the Pink Room was.

"Please bring back my daddy to me."

The voice faded away, but someone continued to hum the melody of the familiar song. At first it sounded almost cheerful. But then the melody faltered, and when it was picked up again, the voice sounded sad.

"My . . . daddy," the singer got out before starting to cry.

A boom of thunder made Jen jump. Rain thrummed on the roof.

"My daddy is over the ocean," the voice said, stronger than before. "My daddy is over the sea."

A chill wind swept around Jen. She smelled salty air.

"My daddy is over the ocean."

The voice was almost a howl now. In the darkness at the end of the hall, Jen thought she saw the door to the Pink Room open inward. Pale moonlight filled the doorway and spilled onto the hallway carpet along with the sound of more rain.

Jen wished her aunt would hear what was happening and come out of her bedroom. But Liv apparently could sleep through it all. Again, Jen considered the possibility that maybe she was dreaming. *Wake up, wake up, wake up*, she told herself. But she knew she was already awake. Whatever was happening didn't make sense. It was pretty much impossible. But it was definitely real.

The singing began again, and this time it was accompanied by music, a kind of mechanical, tinkling sound. "My daddy is over the ocean. My daddy is over the sea. My daddy is over the ocean. Please bring back my daddy to me."

This time, instead of stopping or fading away, the voice kept going. "Bring back, bring back, oh, bring back my daddy to me, to me. Bring back, bring back, oh, bring back my daddy to me."

As the music continued to play, repeating the song again, the girl started to sob. Her cries filled the hallway like the sound of the rain and thunder. The louder they were, the faster the music played, until it became wild and out of control. It was a terrible sound, and Jen wished it would stop. But it continued on, until the girl's crying and the distorted music became a storm of their own, a storm that raged through the third-floor hallway of Pratchett House. Jen put her hands over her ears.

"Stop it!" she shouted.

The lights in the hall came on, startling her with their sudden brightness. Aunt Liv appeared at the top of the stairs, coming up from the floor below. "What's the matter?" she asked, sounding worried.

Jen stared at her, shocked. "You weren't in your room?" she asked.

"No," her aunt said. "I was in the workroom."

"In the dark?" said Jen.

"What?" said Liv. "No, not in the dark. Are you okay?"

"The power was off," Jen explained.

Aunt Liv looked surprised. "Really?" she said. "It wasn't off downstairs. Are you sure?"

Jen nodded. "Didn't you hear the music? And the girl singing?"

"I didn't hear a thing," said Liv. "Not until you shouted.

You scared me half to death. I thought something horrible had happened."

Something horrible did *happen*, Jen thought, but she kept it to herself.

"What did you hear?" Liv asked.

"Someone was singing 'My Bonnie Lies over the Ocean,'" Jen told her. "Only they changed the words."

To her surprise, Aunt Liv laughed. "I think I can explain that," she said.

She walked into the Pink Room. A few seconds later, Jen heard the same music that had been playing earlier. Then her aunt walked back into the hallway carrying something. A Nix followed her out of the room and ran down the stairs.

"It's a music box," she said, holding it up for Jen to see.

Jen walked down the hall to where Liv was standing. The music box in her hand looked old. It continued to play "My Bonnie Lies over the Ocean" for a little while, then slowed down until it stopped.

"Is that what you heard?" Liv asked.

Jen nodded. But that wasn't quite true. She'd also heard someone singing. And it didn't explain why the music had become so out of control at the end. Or the sounds of the storm. But she'd mentioned a storm to her aunt once before and been told she'd made it up. She wasn't going to make that mistake again.

"I was told that Captain Pratchett brought this back for Pearl on one of his trips," Liv said. "It sits on the dresser in there."

"What would make it start playing now?" Jen asked her.

"That's a good question," said Liv. "Old things can behave strangely sometimes. Maybe I wound it up at some point but the mechanism that triggers it to start playing was stuck. A Nix was in there. Maybe it bumped it. I don't know. But at least the mystery has been solved."

Jen nodded again, but only to make Aunt Liv feel better. As far as she was concerned, the mystery was still a mystery. She waited as Liv returned the music box to the Pink Room and came back out.

"Sorry I scared you," she told Liv.

"It's okay," Liv said. "I didn't sleep very well the first few nights I was in this house either. There's a lot of history here, and not all of it pleasant. If you were thinking about that, maybe it made you have bad dreams. Are you okay to go back to your room?"

"Sure," Jen said, trying to sound like she meant it. "I'll see you in the morning."

She went back to her room and shut the door. At least it was warm again in there now. Whatever had caused it to be so cold was over with. In fact, the whole thing was starting to feel like maybe Jen *had* imagined it. Not the music. That had definitely been real. But the music box starting to play on its own was a good explanation for that.

As for the singing, it was possible that hearing the music had made Jen think about the words to a familiar song and hear them when they weren't really there.

Except, she reminded herself, the person singing had changed the words slightly. They hadn't sung about someone called Bonnie. They had sung about someone they called Daddy.

Then again, she had recently heard the story about Pearl Pratchett and her father. Like Aunt Liv had said, that could have been stuck in her mind and become part of what she was imagining.

Everything she told herself made sense and explained what she'd heard. It was logical, believable, and rational. The only problem was, she knew it wasn't true. She *had* heard singing. She *had* felt the cold air and smelled the sea. There *had* been something very, very strange happening on the third floor of Pratchett House. And Jen was pretty sure whatever it was, it was somehow connected to the Pink Room, where the portrait of Pearl Pratchett hung. Where Pearl had died.

She sat down on her bed and thought about the situation. She knew that if she could ask her parents for advice, they would tell her to go about things in a scientific way. That meant examining the evidence for clues to explain what she couldn't yet explain. Already, Aunt Liv had given her at least one explanation for the music she'd heard—the music box. And she had to admit that she *did* have a very active imagination.

"And do you believe in ghosts?" she asked herself out loud.

"No," she said firmly.

"Then that's that. Something started the music box playing and you made up the rest in your head because of the stories Joe and Aunt Liv told you about Pearl Pratchett and her father. Okay?"

She hesitated a moment before saying, "Okay."

She got back into bed and lay there. She told herself she was trying to go back to sleep. But she knew what she was really doing.

She was waiting to hear the music again.

6

Jen waited impatiently for the morning ferry to dock and for Joe to get off.

"Sorry," Joe said when he saw her standing there. "I don't have any mail for you today."

"That's okay," Jen said. "It's you I want to talk to."

"Uh-oh," Joe said. "Am I in trouble?"

"Not yet," said Jen.

"Am I *going* to be?" Joe asked, looking worried.

"I hope not," said Jen. She looked around to see if anyone might be listening, then said quietly, "Can you get into the old lighthouse?"

Joe grinned. "Sure can," he said. Then he looked at her suspiciously. "Why?"

"I'll tell you on the way," Jen said. "How much time do you have?"

"Actually, I'm here until the afternoon ferry goes back," Joe said. "I'm helping Uncle Alex at the diner later."

"Great," Jen said. "Let's go."

She'd walked down to the dock, telling Aunt Liv she wanted to explore the island a little more after breakfast. That part was true. What she hadn't told her was that the part of the island she wanted to explore was one she knew she wasn't supposed to be anywhere near.

"Why do you want to get inside the lighthouse?" Joe asked as they walked up the hill.

Jen had been trying to decide how much she wanted to tell Joe about the strange thing that had happened at Pratchett House the night before. She wasn't worried that he would make fun of her. She knew him well enough already to know he wouldn't do that. She was more worried that he would believe there really was a ghost in her aunt's house when she was trying to prove exactly the opposite. Finally, she told him about the music and the singing. It seemed like the right thing to do when she was asking him to help her do something she knew she shouldn't be doing.

"You think you heard the ghost of Pearl Pratchett singing?" he said, sounding more excited than Jen liked. "That's so cool!"

"I didn't say anything about a ghost," Jen reminded him.

"Then who was doing the singing?" Joe asked.

"I don't know," said Jen. "I think I just imagined it."

"Really?" said Joe, clearly not believing her.

Jen hesitated before answering him. "No," she admitted. "I think I really heard it."

"So, it *was* a ghost," Joe said happily. "Wait. That still doesn't explain why you want to get inside the lighthouse."

"I just want to look around," Jen said. "You told me that Pearl Pratchett and Arthur Crunk were close. That he blamed himself for her death."

"Yeah," Joe agreed.

"I want to see where he lived," Jen said. She sighed. "I'm looking for clues, I guess. I have no idea what those clues might be. But I have to start somewhere, and the creepy old lighthouse that everyone says is haunted seems like a good place to look first. Chester McKiser told me to stay away from it, though."

"He tells everyone that," Joe said. "He thinks the whole island belongs to him."

"But the lighthouse does, right?"

"My uncle says it belongs to history," Joe replied.

"Somehow I don't think that will get us out of trouble if we're caught in there," Jen said.

"Then we won't get caught," said Joe. "Besides, Chester isn't usually there. It will be fine."

When they reached the lighthouse, they were still the

only ones around. Joe walked up to the lighthouse and opened the door.

"I thought it was locked!" Jen exclaimed. She'd expected him to know some kind of trick for getting in.

"Everybody thinks that," said Joe. "But the lock hasn't worked in years."

"I could have done this myself," Jen said as she stepped inside.

"But it wouldn't have been as much fun," Joe said, coming in after her and shutting the door. Then he stopped and looked at Jen. "When you thought it was locked, why did you think I would know how to get in, anyway?"

"I don't know," Jen said as she looked around the room they were in. "Getting into places you're not supposed to be in seems like something you'd be good at."

"I want to be mad about that, but you're right," Joe said.

"It was a compliment," Jen said, laughing. "I mean, you seem to know a lot of useful stuff. So, tell me about this place."

"Well, there's not much to it," Joe said. "A couple of rooms down here where the lighthouse keeper lived, and then there's the tower with the light."

"How long ago did they shut it up?"

"Long time," Joe said. "Fifty, sixty years. When they put the automated light in the bay."

To Jen's disappointment, there wasn't anything very interesting in the first room. In fact, it looked like someone had mostly been using it as a place to store things like a push mower and some garden tools. She walked through a doorway and into the next room. This one wasn't any more interesting, although there was an old cookstove in one corner and a pair of old boots that looked cracked and oily enough that they might have belonged to someone a couple of hundred years ago.

"The steps to the tower are through there," Joe said, indicating a doorway.

"Might as well see what's up there," said Jen, heading for the stairs. She climbed the narrow stone steps as they corkscrewed to the left, going up at a steep incline. Finally, she emerged into a round room. In the center was the old light itself, basically a large metal drum with a shattered bulb in the center. Jen was actually more interested in the windows that encircled the entire room, offering a fantastic view of the island and the surrounding ocean.

"Imagine being up here during a storm?" she said.

"I have," Joe told her. "A couple of times I've come up here and spent the night in my sleeping bag. I wanted to get an idea of what it might have been like for old Arthur. Also, I kind of wanted to see if his ghost showed up. They say he only appears during storms. Never when it's nice weather."

"But you didn't see him?"

Joe shook his head.

Jen was looking out the windows that faced the house below when she gasped. "Someone's coming!"

Joe joined her at the window. "That's Chester," he said. "And Maddie."

"I'm not sure which one I want to run into less," said Jen. "What do we do?"

"There's only one way in and out," Joe told her. "All we can do is hope they don't come up here."

Jen felt sick to her stomach. If Chester found her in the lighthouse, she knew he would use it against Aunt Olivia somehow. And if Maddie knew about it, that would make everything even worse. Plus, she'd dragged Joe into it, and he would surely get in trouble too.

They heard some noise downstairs as the front door opened. Then voices floated up the stairs. They were surprisingly loud and clear.

"The tower acts like an amplifier," Joe whispered quietly to Jen. "Try not to make any noise."

Jen nodded, then went back to eavesdropping.

"I don't know why that door was open," Chester McKiser said angrily. "Someone must have broken the lock."

"The lock hasn't worked in like two years, Uncle

Chester," Maddie said. "I guess you really care a lot about this place if you didn't know that."

"Don't get smart with me," Chester snapped. "I can make my offer to someone else."

"I don't even know what your offer is," said Maddie. "And why did we have to come here for you to make it?"

"Because it's the only place I can be sure there aren't spying eyes and ears," Chester said.

Jen looked at Joe, who grinned. Despite the danger they were in, he was obviously excited that they were accidentally hearing something Chester McKiser didn't want them to.

"Well, we're here," Maddie said. "What is it?"

"You know I want Pratchett House so I can turn it into a hotel," Chester said.

"Everybody knows that," said Maddie. "But Olivia will never sell it to you."

Chester snorted. "You islanders are all the same," he said. "Too stubborn for your own good."

"You used to be an islander too, remember?" said Maddie. "You and my father grew up here."

"And I was smart enough to get away as soon as I could," Chester said. "But I'm also smart enough to know that there's still money to be made here. *If* I can get Olivia to sell. That's why I have a new plan."

"Oh?" Maddie said. "What is it?"

"You want to go to college, right?" McKiser said instead of answering her question.

"Someday, yeah," said Maddie.

"And in the meantime, your family could use some money," McKiser continued. "Nobody makes much from lobstering. So, I have an offer. You help me and I'll give you enough money to go to school and take care of your family."

"What do I have to do?"

"Something I'm not capable of doing," Chester said. "Be nice. Specifically, I want you to befriend Olivia's niece, the one who's here for the summer."

Jen cringed as she heard Maddie snort. "I've already met her," she said in a very *not* friendly tone.

"Well, meet her again," said Chester. "Become her friend. Become her *best* friend."

"Why?" Maddie asked. "How is that going to help you get what you want?"

"It's going to get you into Pratchett House," Chester said. "Don't all girls like to have sleepovers?"

"No," Maddie said. "Not all girls."

"She seems like the sort who does," said Chester. "Once you become her dearest friend on the island, you'll invite yourself over. Once that happens, let me know and I'll tell you what to do next."

"How am I supposed to explain to the Toms where all this money is coming from?" Maddie said.

"It will be a scholarship," Chester explained. "From an unnamed benefactor. My lawyer will handle it all. The Toms will never know it's from me."

"They wouldn't accept it if they did," Maddie informed him.

"Like I said, the islanders are too stubborn for their own good. That's why I'm making this offer to you and not to that Socobasin kid. He's just like his uncle. You're more . . . pragmatic."

Jen glanced at Joe, who was nodding as if he agreed with Chester McKiser.

"So," Chester said. "Do we have a deal?"

There was silence as Maddie seemed to consider the offer. "Sure," she said finally. "We have a deal."

"Wonderful," said Chester. "Now, let's get out of here. I have better things to do with my time than hang out in this dump."

The two of them left, and finally Jen could breathe. "Come on," she said. "We have to tell Aunt Liv what we heard."

"And get in trouble for being here?" Joe said.

"She won't be mad once she hears that Chester and Maddie are up to something."

Joe didn't move. He was thinking. "I still don't think we

should say anything," he said. "It will be our word against theirs, and they'll just deny everything. Then everyone will be mad at us. Let's wait and see what they're up to."

"You mean go along with being Maddie's friend?"

Joe nodded. "At least until we get some real proof. That shouldn't take too long."

Jen thought about having to pretend to like Maddie. As far as she was concerned, even an hour was too long. But she also suspected that Joe was right.

"Okay," she said. "I'll do it for Aunt Liv."

7

Jen and Joe waited fifteen minutes, to give Maddie and Chester McKiser time to get far enough away from the lighthouse, then they left. When they reached the place where the road went in two directions, Joe headed back toward the dock and Jen went in the direction of Pratchett House. She walked slowly, thinking about everything they'd heard at the lighthouse and what it might mean. Obviously, Chester had some kind of plan to get Aunt Liv out of her house. But what could it be?

Jen was thinking so much about this question that she didn't even see Maddie coming down the steps of the house just as she was about to walk up them. The two of them collided, making Jen give a little shriek of surprise.

"What are you doing here?" she barked.

"Nothing," Maddie said, sounding like her usual unpleasant self. Then she seemed to remember something and added in a nicer tone, "I mean, I came to see you."

Jen, knowing that only a little while ago Maddie had made a deal with Chester McKiser to pretend to be her friend, crossed her arms over her chest and said, "Why?"

"Because," Maddie said. "I, uh, wanted to invite you to come get lobsters."

"What?" said Jen. "Lobsters?"

"Yeah," Maddie said. "Haven't you ever eaten lobster?"

"Sure," Jen answered. "Lots of times."

This was not actually true. She'd had lobster only once, at a fancy restaurant her parents had taken her to. And she hadn't even ordered it. Her father had, and she'd had a bite of his.

"But have you ever harvested your own lobster right out of the ocean?" asked Maddie.

"No," Jen admitted. "I've never done that."

"Great," Maddie said, sounding more relieved than excited. "Today, you will. Be at my house at eleven. We'll go out with the Toms and have a lobster boil when we get back. Tell your aunt to be at our place around three. She knows where it is. See ya."

She walked off, not waiting for Jen to respond. Jen watched her go, then went up the stairs and into the house. Aunt Liv was in her second-floor workroom.

"We're invited to Maddie's house for a lobster boil," she told Liv. "Actually, *I'm* invited to catch the lobsters for it. You just have to come eat them, I guess."

"That sounds fun," her aunt said. "I told you she'd like you."

Jen made a grunting sound. She wished she could tell Liv that Maddie was only pretending to like her. But that would mean explaining how she knew that, so she kept the information to herself and instead asked, "What are you doing?"

"Restringing this doll," Liv said. "Want to learn how?"

"It looks complicated," Jen said.

"Everything looks complicated until you learn how to do it," said her aunt. "Watch."

Jen observed while Liv measured out several lengths of elastic cord, then tied them into loops and used them to connect the ceramic arms and legs of the doll she was working on to the body by passing the cords through openings in the torso and securing them to metal hooks in the body parts. "See?" Liv said as she worked. "It's really a matter of getting the lengths right so that the tension holds everything together properly. Want to try doing this next one?"

Jen cut a piece of cord and went to work. Aunt Liv showed her how to measure it out and get it exactly the right length so that the doll's joints weren't too loose or too tight. It took Jen a couple of tries to get it just right, but eventually she had both the arms and legs on.

"Good job!" Aunt Liv said after inspecting her work.

"You're a born doll doctor. I might have to move you up from the mailroom sooner than I thought."

Jen laughed. "Doctor Jen, doll surgeon, reporting for duty," she said.

Aunt Liv looked at the clock. "You'd better get going," she said. "You don't want to be late for lobster hunting."

Jen sighed. She'd forgotten about the lobsters. And about having to spend time with that traitor Maddie. She wished she could get out of it. But she needed to figure out what Maddie was planning, and this seemed like a good way to get started on that. If Maddie was pretending to be her friend, she could do the same thing.

"Guess I'll see you around three," she said.

"Tell Tom I'll bring potato salad," said Liv.

"Which one?" Jen asked. "There are two, right?"

"Either one," said Liv.

Jen left Pratchett House and walked into town. Liv had told her how to find Maddie's house, and she arrived to find Maddie standing beside a small dock. Tied to the dock was a boat. And on the boat were two men. They both had dark hair and beards, but one was small and wiry while the other was quite large.

"Hey there!" the smaller one said, waving. "You must be Jen. I'm Little Tom. That fella is Big Tom." The man had a strong accent, so *Tom* sounded more like *Tahm* to Jen's ears.

"Nice to meet you," Jen said. "Aunt Liv said to tell you she's bringing potato salad."

"Oh, that's fine," said Big Tom. "She makes a good potato salad."

Maddie came over holding an orange life vest, which she handed to Jen. "In case you fall over," she said, somehow making it sound like a threat.

Jen put the vest on and secured it, then climbed onto the boat with Little Tom's help. She sat down where Maddie showed her to sit, and tried to stay out of the way as the Toms backed the boat away from the dock.

"Since we're just getting lobsters for dinner, we're taking

the small boat," Maddie explained. "Normally they take that one." She pointed at a much larger boat anchored farther from the dock.

They weren't able to talk much more, as the sound of the motor made hearing anything difficult. That was all right with Jen, though, since she had no idea what to talk to Maddie about. Knowing that she was only being nice to Jen because Chester was paying her made it hard to think of her in any positive way. She wondered what the Toms would think if they knew what Maddie was up to.

Little Tom drove the boat, heading for a buoy that was bobbing up and down on the surface. It was painted turquoise blue with bright pink and white stripes. Jen knew that everyone with a license to harvest lobster had buoys painted with their own unique colors to identify which traps were theirs. This one must be the Toms'. She wondered if the pretty colors meant anything in particular or if they just liked them.

Little Tom stopped the boat next to the buoy. "All

right," Big Tom said. "Let's see if we got anything."

He reached over and grabbed the rope attached to the buoy. Pulling on it, he hauled the lobster trap up from where it sat on the ocean floor below. Jen waited expectantly until the top of the trap broke the surface. Little Tom leaned over and grabbed one end of the trap and helped Big Tom lift it into the boat.

The trap was a big wire rectangle separated into several areas by netting. A bag of something fishy-smelling dangled in one corner. Jen looked more closely and saw that it actually *was* fish, or at least pieces of fish, including a head that stared back at her with dead, glassy eyes. She guessed that was the bait that lured the lobsters into the trap.

"Parlor's empty," Big Tom said. "Back in she goes."

"That means there are no lobsters in the area where they get trapped trying to get out," Maddie explained to Jen.

Big Tom dropped the trap back over the side, then motored the boat to the next buoy. This trap too was empty.

Jen wasn't sure if she was disappointed or if she was happy that no lobsters had been caught.

When the third trap came up, the Toms cheered. There were two lobsters in the trap. Little Tom took them out, measured them to make sure they were legal size to keep, and put them into a bucket filled with seawater. The bucket sat between Maddie and Jen, so Jen watched the lobsters as the Toms moved on to the next trap.

"You're thinking about setting them free, aren't you?" Maddie asked.

"Kind of," said Jen. "How did you know?"

"Because I used to think the same thing when I first started helping with the pots," Maddie said. "I felt bad for them, knowing what was going to happen to them."

Jen nodded. That was exactly what she had been thinking herself.

"One time I did it," Maddie continued. "I dumped an entire cooler of them over the side. A whole day's catch."

"Were the Toms mad?" Jen asked.

Maddie shook her head. "They never get mad," she said. "But it was a long time before they let me come with them again."

Jen laughed. Then she remembered that she was supposed to dislike Maddie. She *did* dislike Maddie. But it was still a funny story. And the fact that Maddie had wanted to help the lobsters was pretty cool.

Little Tom stopped the boat again. "Want to help with this one?" he asked Jen.

"Sure!" Jen said. Despite feeling kind of bad for the lobsters, she was also enjoying watching the traps come up and seeing what was in them. She joined Big Tom at the side of the boat and took the rope he handed her. She pulled, feeling the trap lift up somewhere below. It was much heavier than she expected, but Big Tom did most of the work.

Her arms ached as she pulled and pulled. Finally, she saw the trap through the dark brown water. And she thought she saw something inside it.

"Looks like we've got something!" Big Tom said.

When the trap was over the side and on the floor of the boat, Jen looked more closely. Sure enough, one side of it was filled with a mass of something green.

"It's just seaweed," Maddie said from over her shoulder.

"No, there's something else," Big Tom told her.

He reached into the trap and pulled out the clump of seaweed, placing it on the floor beside the trap. The seaweed was indeed wrapped around something. Big Tom peeled the strands away. Tiny crabs scuttled out of the seaweed nest and sat in the puddle of water on the boat floor.

"What is it?" Little Tom asked.

"Almost there," said Big Tom. He pulled more seaweed away.

Looking up at them was a head. A doll's head. It was about half the size of a real head, with blue painted eyes and a pink mouth. Gold hair was attached to it, and the sodden strands clung to the cheeks. A large crack ran across the face, with a chip at the forehead.

"That looks old," Maddie said.

Big Tom picked the head up and held it in his hand. "How in the world did it get inside the trap?" he said.

No one answered that question. But Jen certainly was thinking about it as she stared at the doll's face. Because that face looked very familiar to her.

It belonged to the doll that Pearl Pratchett was holding in her portrait.

8

"It's old. Very old."

Aunt Liv turned the head over and showed them a design stamped on the back of the neck.

"This is the mark of a London doll maker named Elder-Fox. See how it's a fox head?"

Jen peered closely at the mark and saw that it was indeed a fox looking out at her, with what looked to be a twig in its mouth.

"That's an elder branch it's holding," Liv explained. "Sefina Fox and Gregory Elder were the doll makers who founded the company."

"Can you tell when it was made?" Maddie asked.

They were in the yard at Maddie's house. There was a fire going in a circle of stones. Rising up over the pit was a tripod made from thick metal rods, and suspended from the center on a chain was a cast-iron cooking pot. Inside the pot were the lobsters they had caught earlier in the day, as well as a bunch of clams, salt potatoes, and corn on the cob. It was all steaming together.

Everyone was seated near the firepit in camp chairs, waiting for supper to be ready. At the moment, though, they were distracted by listening to what Liv could tell them about the head they'd found in the lobster trap.

"It had to be sometime between 1798 and 1833," Liv said. "Those were the only years Elder-Fox produced dolls."

"It's in amazing shape for something so old," Little Tom remarked.

"Cold water can preserve things," said Liv. "Even so, the fact that the hair is still intact is astonishing."

Jen asked the question she knew everyone was thinking. "Is it the head from Pearl Pratchett's doll?"

Aunt Liv shrugged. "I can't say for certain. For one thing, we don't have the body of that doll. It went missing after Pearl's death. But the age and maker would fit with what we know about it."

"That head has been in the water for two hundred years?" Maddie said, sounding as if she didn't believe it.

"It's unlikely," Liv agreed. "But it's possible. They've found glass bottles and other items intact from shipwrecks much older than this doll head."

"That still doesn't explain how it ended up in one of our traps," Big Tom said. "Pretty hard for water motion to sweep it in there."

Nobody had a suggestion for how that might have happened.

"What are you going to do with it?" Maddie asked.

"Me?" Liv said. "It's not mine. If anything, it should be in a museum."

"Too bad the island doesn't have one," Little Tom said.

"We would if Chester would deed the lighthouse to the island instead of trying to make a profit from it," said Big Tom.

Jen glanced at Maddie and saw that she had a strange expression on her face. Jen wondered how she felt about the Toms saying these things.

"You could restore it, couldn't you?" Jen asked her aunt. "Fix the hair and clean up the missing paint?"

Aunt Liv nodded. "I wouldn't do too much to it, actually. That would ruin the historic value of it. But the hair could definitely use some work."

Big Tom, who had gone over to check on the lobster boil, announced that it was ready. The doll head was (mostly) forgotten as everyone picked up plates and went over to the pot, where Big Tom scooped out lobster, clams, potatoes, and corn for each of them. Then they gathered around the picnic table set up nearby and started to eat. Little Tom showed Jen how to crack the lobster claws and dip the meat into a bowl of melted butter.

"What do you think?" he asked after Jen tried her first bite.

"It's fantastic," Jen said.

"Try a clam," Maddie suggested.

Jen picked up one of the open shells on her plate and pulled the clam out with her fingers. She dipped this in the butter too, then popped it into her mouth. It was salty and a little chewy.

"Delicious!" she said.

"Looks like we've got a Mainer in the making," Big Tom said, laughing.

For the next little while they ate and talked. Then Little Tom brought out a blueberry pie and vanilla ice cream.

"Let me guess," Liv said. "Alex made the pie?"

"Of course," said Little Tom as he cut big slices for everyone. "I gave up making them because I can never get one to come out as good as his. I don't know what we'll do if he ever decides to leave the island and cook somewhere else."

"Alex will never leave Big Rock," Big Tom said. "He's as much a part of this place as the puffins and seals are."

"True," Little Tom said. "But it gets harder and harder to make a living here. You know that. Not much here for young people."

Jen looked over at Maddie, who concentrated on her pie and didn't say anything. When they were done, Jen helped carry the dishes into the house, where they put them in the kitchen sink.

"This was fun," Jen told Maddie. "Thanks for inviting me." Although partly she was doing this to make Maddie think she was clueless about Maddie's reasons for asking her over, she also really had enjoyed herself.

"You can stay over," Maddie said, surprising Jen. "I mean, if you want."

Jen hesitated. She didn't want to. But she also thought it might be smart to make Maddie think she liked her.

"Sure," she said before she could talk herself out of it. "As long as Aunt Liv says it's okay."

"Of course!" Liv said a minute later when Jen asked her. "I'm glad the two of you are becoming friends."

Jen nodded. "Me too," she said, wishing she could tell her aunt the truth about what was going on with Maddie.

Liv left and Jen found herself in Maddie's bedroom.

"I'll get you a toothbrush," Maddie said, leaving Jen alone.

Jen looked around the room. The thing she noticed most were the books. They were everywhere—overflowing the shelves of the two bookcases, in piles on the floor, stacked on the corner of the dresser. A lot of them were horror novels like the one Jen had seen Maddie reading on the rock at the beach. But not all of them. Jen noticed a couple of titles that sounded like romance books. And there was a stack of handbooks for role-playing games.

Tucked into the edge of the mirror hanging over Maddie's dresser were some photos. Most of them looked recent and showed Maddie doing things with the Toms. But one was older. Maddie was younger in it, and she was standing between Big Tom and someone who looked a lot like

Little Tom but without a beard. Maddie walked in as Jen was looking at the picture.

"You look really happy here," Jen said.

Maddie laughed. "That was at Palace Playland," she said. "It's an amusement park in Old Orchard Beach. The Toms took me for my ninth birthday."

"Little Tom looks different without the beard," Jen said.

"Yeah," Maddie agreed. She smiled. "But always like Little Tom."

Jen pointed at the bookcase. "Have you read all of those?"

Maddie nodded. "There's not a lot else to do here," she said. "Anyway, I want to be a writer. Someday. When I get out of here."

"You don't want to stay on Big Rock?" Jen asked.

"Not forever," Maddie said. "I'm not going to be a lob-sterman or work at the diner. I want to see what else there is besides this island."

"I guess it's different when you grow up here," Jen said. "To me it's all new and exciting."

"That wears off," Maddie said, sounding more like the girl Jen had met on the beach. "I can't wait to live somewhere else."

"Why so many horror books?" Jen asked her. "Do you like being scared?"

"It was kind of an accident," Maddie answered. "Stephen King is from Maine, and a lot of tourists read him while they're here, so the used bookstore on the mainland is filled with his books. They sell them for like fifty cents each, which is why I started buying them. Also, people who saw me reading them on the ferry kept telling me I was too young to read them, which made me want to read them even more."

Jen laughed at that. It sounded like Maddie, all right.

"I really do like his books," Maddie continued. "But I like all kinds of stories."

"Finding that head in the lobster trap today is like something out of a story," Jen said.

"It was definitely weird," Maddie said. "Especially since your aunt lives in Pratchett House. Does that scare you?"

Jen thought about telling Maddie what she'd experienced in Pratchett House. Then she reminded herself that Maddie was only pretending to be interested so that Jen would invite her over. Remembering that made her angry again.

"No," she said. "It's just a house. It's not like it's haunted."

"All those dolls, though," Maddie said. "Dolls kind of creep me out."

Now it felt like Maddie was *trying* to scare Jen. Jen wasn't about to let her think she had succeeded. "They're just dolls," she said.

"Sure," Maddie said. "It's not like they come alive at night or anything, right?"

"Right," said Jen.

"Or watch you while you sleep," said Maddie.

"Definitely not."

"And if they *did*, I'm sure they wouldn't be thinking about turning *you* into a doll too, so that you could all live together forever in that big dollhouse," Maddie said, grinning.

Jen looked at her. "Okay," she said. "That was creepy. Stephen King better watch out."

"Come on," Maddie said. "Let's see if there's some more pie in the kitchen. That will make you forget all about scary dolls."

Maddie followed her out of the room. But she knew Maddie was wrong.

Now she was thinking about dolls even more than before.

9

"Good work," Joe told Jen. "You're like a secret agent!"

It was the day after Jen's sleepover at Maddie's house. Joe had driven a golf cart up to Pratchett House to deliver a couple of dolls and some mail, and he and Jen were sitting on the front porch. Two Nixes were lying in the sun, and Joe was scratching one of them behind the ears while he and Jen talked.

"It felt weird," Jen told him. "Like, I know she's only being nice to me because she's trying to get something. But it was also sort of fun."

Joe made a face. "I can't imagine spending time with Maddie is fun," he said.

"I know," Jen agreed. "But it kind of was. Like, when she wasn't trying so hard to be the way she usually is."

"Remember, she's trying to get you to trust her," Joe reminded Jen. "So she can get into Pratchett House and do whatever it is Chester wants her to do."

"Well, she's getting in," Jen said. "I invited her over tonight."

"What?" Joe exclaimed. "Why?"

"Because that's what you do when someone has had you spend the night at their house," said Jen. "You have them over to your house. It would look weird if I didn't ask her. Besides, Aunt Liv said I should."

"Okay," Joe said. "But make sure you keep an eye on her."

"I will," Jen promised. "Hey, you could come over too, you know."

Joe made a face. "A sleepover with a couple of girls?" he said.

"I bet Maddie would love to tell you one of her scary stories," Jen teased.

"No, thanks," Joe said.

The door to the house opened and Aunt Liv came out carrying a box. "Thanks for waiting, Joe," she said. "I meant to have this ready this morning, but the paint on the face wasn't completely dry."

Joe took the box Liv handed him and walked down the steps to the golf cart. He put the box in the back. "I'll see you later," he said, waving.

When he was gone, Jen went inside with her aunt. Aunt Liv was looking at the mail Joe had brought. She opened one of the envelopes and took out a piece of paper. Jen watched as she read it and a frown appeared on her face.

"Everything okay?" Jen asked.

"What?" Liv said. "Oh, yes. Fine. Hey, have you thought about what you and Maddie might want to do tonight?"

It sounded to Jen like her aunt was trying to change the subject. "I thought we could make cookies or something," she said. "Maybe watch a movie."

"Good idea," Liv said a little too brightly. "We have stuff to make chocolate chip cookies, I think. And there are a bunch of DVDs to pick from. What kind of movies do you think Maddie likes?"

"Scary ones," Jen answered instantly.

"I'm afraid I don't have any scary ones," Aunt Liv said. "I'm a big baby when it comes to those. I like my movies with lots of laughs and maybe a few tears."

"I'm sure we'll find something," Jen assured her.

"Great," Liv said. "Well, I'm going to get back to work."

She turned and walked out of the room. Then Jen noticed that she had dropped something. A piece of paper lay on the floor, where a Nix was poking at it with one paw.

"I think that might be important," Jen told the cat, retrieving the paper.

Although she knew she shouldn't, she looked at the paper in her hand. It seemed to be a letter from Aunt Liv's bank. Jen scanned it, and suddenly she knew why her aunt had looked upset. It was a letter informing her that she was behind on her mortgage and needed to make a pretty big payment soon or she might lose Pratchett House.

Was Aunt Liv having money problems? It seemed so. And there was no way Jen could ask her about it since she shouldn't have looked at the letter in the first place. Now she didn't know what to do.

She took the letter into the kitchen, folded it up, and set it on the counter. Hopefully, Aunt Liv would think she had put it there herself. Then Jen went out and did some weeding in the garden, trying to distract herself from this new worry. She didn't know what she could possibly do to help Aunt Liv. And she couldn't even contact her parents to ask them for their advice. All she could do was pull the weeds from between the rows of green beans.

She was almost done when Maddie appeared at the end of a row.

"Hey," she said. "Having fun?"

Jen stood up, stretching the sore muscles in her legs.

"Not really," she said. She wished she could tell Maddie what was worrying her. Then she remembered that they weren't really friends.

Maddie held something up. "I wasn't sure what movies you had, so I brought *Spirited Away*," she said. "Do you like Hayao Miyazaki movies?"

"I love them!" Jen said, forgetting for a moment that she was still upset. "I think *Howl's Moving Castle* is my favorite. Especially Calcifer."

"He's definitely the best part of that one," Maddie said. "I'm glad you like those movies too."

There was an awkward silence as they both stood there, not saying anything. Jen was thinking that she and Maddie had more in common than she'd initially believed. She wondered if Maddie was thinking the same thing, and if it made her feel funny too.

"Let's go inside and see what we have for dinner," she said.

Aunt Liv was already in the kitchen when they went into

the house. Jen noticed that the letter wasn't on the counter where she'd left it. She wondered if her aunt suspected that she'd read it. She didn't seem quite as distracted as she had earlier.

"Hey there," she said, sounding like her old self. "I thought we would make homemade pizzas for dinner. We have a lot of tomatoes and herbs from the garden, and I have some fantastic fresh mozzarella I picked up at the farmers' market on the mainland last week. We could also do one with mushrooms, goat cheese, and arugula if you're feeling adventurous."

"Sounds good to me," Maddie said.

"Great," Liv said. "The dough is rising, so we can chop up vegetables and get everything else ready."

As the three of them worked on the pizzas, Jen thought about how she *ought* to be having a wonderful time. But she couldn't stop thinking about how her friendship with Maddie wasn't real. And now there was the thing about Aunt Liv maybe losing the house. These thoughts filled her mind like storm clouds, preventing her from enjoying what they were doing.

Still, she was able to act like nothing was wrong, rolling out the dough that Aunt Liv had made and spreading it with sauce and toppings. She imagined Joe congratulating her on being a great spy, which sort of helped.

After dinner, she and Maddie did dishes while Liv went back to work. Then they made the chocolate chip cookies. They didn't even wait for them to cool before putting some on a plate and taking them up to Aunt Liv. The rest they put on a plate for themselves, carrying them into the room where the TV and DVD player were.

Jen pretended to pay attention to the movie, but the whole time it was on she was thinking about her problems. By the time the movie was over, she still hadn't thought of any way to help her aunt. Then she realized she had another problem. She hadn't asked Aunt Liv where Maddie should sleep. And now her aunt had gone to bed.

Besides her own room, the only other bedroom was the

Pink Room. Thinking about having to sleep in there sent a chill through Jen, but Maddie didn't know anything about the room's history. Maybe if she didn't tell Maddie too much about it, it would be fine. Before she could change her mind, Jen took Maddie up there and opened the door.

"Wow," Maddie said when she went inside. "This is a *lot* of pink." Then she noticed the portrait on the wall. She went over and inspected it. "Is that Pearl? And is that the doll? The head we found looks just like that."

"I know," Jen said, feeling a little anxious about the conversation. "Weird, huh?"

"Super weird," Maddie said. "Was this her room?"

"I think maybe it was," said Jen. She didn't want to say for sure, as she didn't want Maddie to be freaked out about it.

But Maddie seemed excited, not scared. "I bet it was," she said as she sat down on the bed. "Maybe her ghost will visit me tonight."

Jen, thinking about the strange experiences she'd had in

the house, forced a laugh. "If she does, tell her not to wake me up, okay? I'll see you in the morning. Good night."

"Good night," Maddie said. "I had fun tonight."

"Me too," Jen said.

She left Maddie to get ready for bed and headed for the Yellow Room. Conflicting thoughts swirled around in her head as she brushed her teeth and got into bed herself. Would Maddie experience anything weird in the Pink Room? Would she hear noises, or someone singing? And if she did, would she be afraid? Part of her wanted to get Maddie and tell her to come sleep in the Yellow Room with her. Then she reminded herself that Maddie was there to spy on her and Aunt Liv. That made her feel a little better about putting Maddie in the Pink Room.

It took Jen a while to fall asleep, but eventually she did. When she woke up again, it wasn't because she heard a storm, or singing. It was because she was dreaming about eating a chocolate chip cookie. She could practically taste it. So when she woke up and remembered that there were cookies on the kitchen counter, she decided to go downstairs and get one. *Maybe two*, she thought as she opened her door.

She crept downstairs as quietly as she could, leaving the lights off so that she wouldn't accidentally wake anyone up. She went into the kitchen, where the plate of cookies was waiting for her. She picked one up, took a bite, and was savoring the delicious chocolate when she heard a noise in the other room.

Poking her head out of the kitchen, she saw a beam of light coming down the stairs. Then she heard footsteps. A moment later, Maddie appeared.

Jen didn't say anything. Instead, she went back into the kitchen and continued to eat her cookie. Why was Maddie creeping around Pratchett House? Jen knew the answer to that. She was spying.

She heard Maddie moving around in the other room. Then she heard the sound of a door opening. *Maddie's going downstairs*, she thought. *Into the basement.*

Jen went into the living room, just in time to see the

glow from Maddie's flashlight disappear as she descended the stairs. Before she could talk herself out of it, Jen followed. She hesitated at the top of the stairs until Maddie was in the cellar, then crept after her. Her heart pounded as she worried about Maddie catching her. Then she reminded herself that Maddie was the one sneaking around, not her. If Maddie saw her, she would just ask her what *she* was doing!

At the bottom of the stairs, she paused, staying in the darkness so she wouldn't be seen. Maddie walked around the room, shining her flashlight on the workbenches. The glass eyes on the dolls that were lined up there sparkled as the light passed over them. Then a jumble of disembodied arms and legs appeared, scattered over the workbench.

"Yeah, that's not creepy at all," Maddie said. Then she laughed. "Hope I'm not interrupting a doll party or anything."

She kept moving, examining the shelves of jars. The light shined through the liquid in the jars, making the tomatoes and beans inside glow eerily. Finally, Maddie went to the door that led outside and opened it. "Olivia really should keep this locked," she said. "Somebody might sneak in this way."

A sudden thumping noise made Maddie whirl around. She pointed her light in the direction of the workbench. A doll stared back at her, its eyes unblinking.

"Weren't there four of you lined up there a minute ago?" Maddie asked, moving the light to reveal dolls standing on either side of the center one.

The thumping noise came again. This time, Maddie let out a gasp and dropped the flashlight. It went out. Jen heard something moving around, and assumed it was Maddie looking for the light.

"Where are you?" Maddie said, her voice tight. She sounded scared. "Where *are* you?" she said again.

For a second Jen thought Maddie was speaking to her, and almost answered. Then Maddie said, "Found you." This was followed by a clicking sound, and Jen realized that Maddie was trying to turn her flashlight on. But nothing happened.

The thumping sound came again. It almost sounded like something jumping off the workbench to the floor. Jen's brain told her it was most likely a Nix, but she couldn't help thinking about the dolls lined up in the darkness. Being trapped there in the dark with them suddenly felt like the very worst idea.

She heard footsteps and realized that Maddie had decided it was time to get out of the basement too. Jen turned and scurried up the stairs, reaching the top just as Maddie started up behind her. Thankfully, her bare feet made it easier to be quiet as she retreated to the kitchen.

Maddie shut the door behind her and a moment later Jen heard her going back upstairs. Jen stayed in the kitchen. Now that she was out of the cellar, she felt less scared. She took a cookie from the plate and chewed it while she tried to figure out what Maddie had been doing in the cellar. She told herself the cookie was helping her think.

The truth was, though, she had more questions than ever.

10

"I have to run over to the mainland this morning."

Aunt Liv seemed distracted and upset as she gathered her things. Jen was pretty sure she knew what the last-second trip was about—the letter that had come the day before. She also knew she couldn't ask about it.

"Is there anything I can do to help while you're gone?" she asked instead.

"No," Aunt Liv said curtly. Then she took a breath and smiled. "But thank you. I'll be back on the afternoon ferry. You two have a good day."

She hustled out the door, leaving Jen and Maddie alone

in the kitchen. An awkward silence hung over them. Jen was thinking about how she'd caught Maddie sneaking around the house the night before. Again, though, she didn't think she should say anything about it. Not yet, anyway.

"I've got to go too," Maddie said. "I'm supposed to help the Toms with some stuff this morning. Last night was fun. Let's do it again, okay?"

"Sure," Jen said, trying to sound like she was excited by the idea. Really, she was relieved that Maddie was leaving. She had a lot to think about.

When Maddie was gone, Jen went into the kitchen and made herself a bowl of cereal. She took it out to the front porch and sat on the steps to eat it. A couple of Nixes joined her, watching hopefully.

"I wish I could help Aunt Liv," she told the Nixes. "I don't want her to lose this house."

The Nixes blinked at her. One of them licked a paw.

"You're not very helpful," Jen informed them.

She was trying to decide what to do with her day when

Joe came walking up the road to the house. "Hey," he called out. "Your aunt just got on the ferry to the mainland. She seemed like she was in a hurry."

Jen took another bite of cereal and chewed it as she decided what to tell Joe. She knew she shouldn't be discussing her aunt's personal business, but she also trusted Joe to keep a secret. Plus, she really needed to talk about it.

"I think she's going to the bank," she said. Then she told him about the letter.

"That sounds serious," Joe said when she was done.

"Yeah," Jen agreed. "And I can't tell her I know or she'll know I snooped. And there's something else. Maddie was snooping too. In the house last night."

"That's a lot of snooping going on," Joe said, which made Jen laugh and feel a little bit better.

"What do you think I should do?" she asked.

Joe thought for a minute. Then he said, "I think you should come meet Edith."

"Edith?" said Jen. "Who's Edith?"

"The most interesting person on Big Rock Island," Joe told her.

Jen took her cereal bowl into the house, slipped her sneakers on, and rejoined Joe outside. They walked down the road to town, then headed out toward the beach. Jen hoped they wouldn't run into Maddie on the way and was relieved when they didn't. Joe kept going past the end of the beach, walking toward a point of land that stretched out into the ocean. A small house, painted red, sat at the very tip.

"Is that where Edith lives?" Jen asked. "It looks like something out of a fairy tale."

"Edith is kind of like something out of a fairy tale too," Joe remarked as they drew closer to the house.

Jen wondered what he meant by that. Then the door of the house opened, someone stepped out, and she understood. The woman before them had a mass of gray hair that floated around her head like a giant bird's nest. She was dressed in faded overalls patched with a dozen different fabrics, and her left foot was in a brown shoe while the right one was in a red rain boot. She had a tall wooden walking stick in one hand that had a carved bear head at the top.

"Joe!" the woman said happily.

"Hi, Edith," Joe said, giving the woman a hug. "I brought someone to meet you. This is my friend Jen. Olivia is her aunt."

"Hello, new friend!" Edith said, smiling warmly at Jen. "Come in. Come in. I just made coffee. You drink coffee, right?"

"I'm twelve, Edith," Joe said.

"I was drinking coffee when I was six," Edith said, waving a hand in the air. "But you can have root beer. Sit."

The inside of Edith's house looked like a rummage sale. There were things everywhere. Most of the walls were covered in photographs, paintings, and artwork of all kinds. Another was lined with shelves, each one crowded with books, figurines, pieces of wood, and many other things Jen felt like it would take days to look at. They followed Edith into a small kitchen, most of which was taken up by a round table. That's where she and Joe sat while Edith busied herself getting their drinks.

"Did you hear the mermaids singing last night?" Edith asked as she took glasses out of a cupboard and filled them with root beer. "Loud as anything."

Jen looked over at Joe, who raised an eyebrow as if to say, *I told you she was interesting!*

"I didn't," Joe said. "But I wasn't on the island last night."

"You might have heard them," Edith said, setting a glass down in front of Jen and looking at her. "They were loud enough to carry up to the house."

"I didn't either," Jen told her.

"Listen for them tonight," Edith said. "They'll be singing again. On account of the anniversary."

"Anniversary?" Jen said.

"Of the shipwreck," said Edith as she sat down. "The *Amphitrite*." She lifted her mug of coffee and pointed it toward Jen. "That'll be the ship William Pratchett was captain of. Foundered off the rocks out there two hundred years ago next week."

"And the mermaids are singing about it?" Jen asked.

Edith sighed dramactically. "They love to sing about tragedies. The sadder the story, the more beautiful their song about it." She took a sip of coffee. "You know that story, of course. About little Pearl and her doll."

Jen nodded. "I think we found the head to the doll," she said.

Edith's mug hit the table so hard that coffee slopped over the side. "What?" she said.

"The head," Jen said. "It was inside a lobster trap."

"That can't be," Edith said sharply.

"Well, it might not be the actual head," Jen said, afraid she'd upset Edith. "But it looks like the one in the painting."

Edith shook her head from side to side. "No, no, no," she muttered. "She's going to come looking for it."

"Who?" said Jen.

Edith looked at her, her eyes wide. "Pearl," she said. "She's going to come back for her doll. You didn't find the rest of it, did you?"

"No," Jen said. "Just the head."

Edith seemed to calm down a little. "Might not be so bad then. Still, be careful. You never know with ghosts."

She got up and went to the cupboard again, pulling out several little glass jars. She opened them and poured some of the contents from each one into an empty jar, then put a lid on it and shook it. She brought it back to the table and set it in front of Jen. "Sprinkle that around your doorway," she said.

"What's in it?" Jen asked, looking at the jar doubtfully.

"Salt," Edith said. "Graveyard dirt. Some other things ghosts don't care for. It won't harm her, of course. Just keep her from coming in."

"What would happen if she got in?" Jen asked anxiously.

Edith shrugged. "Maybe nothing," she said. "Maybe something. Ghosts are unpredictable. Especially around the time of their deaths. They can forget they're dead and get caught between this world and the next."

Jen picked up the little jar. She wasn't sure she believed anything Edith was saying, but she said, "Thank you."

"We should be getting back," Joe said. "Thanks for the root beer, Edith."

"Next time, you'll be old enough for coffee," Edith said. "And remind me to tell you what the starmen said. It was very interesting."

Joe and Jen left Edith in the kitchen and went outside.

"Starmen?" Jen said as soon as the front door was shut.

"Edith gets visited by UFOs," Joe explained. "Ever since she was a little girl."

"Why am I not surprised?" Jen said. "Mermaids. Ghosts. Why not aliens?"

"Uncle Alex says Edith is probably an alien herself," Joe said. "No one knows anything about her family or where she came from. But she always seems to know everything strange that happens on the island. I thought she might have something to say about Pearl and the doll. That's why I brought you to meet her."

"I like her," Jen said. "And now I have some magic ghost repellent!"

"Are you really going to use it?" Joe asked.

"Maybe," said Jen. "It can't hurt, right?"

"Probably not," Joe agreed. "I mean, it's just salt and dirt."

"I'm more worried about those mermaids," Jen said. "What if we hear them singing and get lured to our deaths? Isn't that what they do?"

"I think only sailors have to worry about that," said Joe.

"You're a sailor," Jen reminded him. "I mean, sort of. You're on the ferry a lot."

"That's true," said Joe. "Maybe I should start wearing earplugs."

"Or you can borrow some of my magic dirt," said Jen. Then a thought came to her. "Do you think the ghost repellent would work on Maddie? I'd like to keep her away too."

"I think it would be easier to just not invite her over again," Joe suggested.

"You're probably right," Jen said. "But maybe I'll sprinkle some on her just in case."

11

"Did you take the doll head off the bench in the workroom?"

Jen stopped slicing the tomato she was cutting up for salad. Aunt Liv stood in the doorway to the kitchen, and she didn't look happy.

"The one from Pearl's doll?" Jen said. "No."

"Well, it's gone," Liv said. Her voice was sharp, and Jen could tell she was upset. She stood there like she was waiting for Jen to admit she had taken it after all.

"Really, I didn't touch it," said Jen. "I haven't even gone in there today. This morning I was with Joe and this afternoon I worked in the garden."

"Maybe Joe took it," Liv said.

"Why would he do that?" asked Jen.

"I don't know!" Liv snapped. "But it's gone, so *someone* took it. I know it was there last night when I went to bed."

Last night. That meant it could have disappeared sometime between then and now. *Like when Maddie was sneaking around the house,* Jen thought.

"Maybe a Nix knocked it off the bench?" Jen suggested.

Liv sighed. "I looked everywhere," she said. "It's not in the room. I'll look again."

She walked away. Jen went back to cutting up the tomato, but she felt bad. Aunt Liv had been in a horrible mood ever since returning from the mainland that afternoon. Jen guessed things hadn't gone well. She'd tried to be helpful, starting dinner without being asked, but it was like her aunt didn't even notice. And now the doll head was missing.

That bothered Jen too. The only person who might have taken it was Maddie. But why would she want it? It didn't make any sense.

She finished making the salad, then checked on the water for the pasta. It had started to boil, so she put the spaghetti in. While that was happening, she got everything else out and set the table. Then she went upstairs to tell Aunt Liv that supper was almost ready. She found her in the workroom, looking under a table.

"Did you find it?" she asked.

"No," Liv said. "It's not here. Someone took it."

"I made dinner," Jen said. "Spaghetti and salad. It's almost ready."

Aunt Liv stood up. "I just don't know who could have taken it," she said as if she hadn't heard what Jen said about supper.

"Everything should be done in a few minutes," Jen said.

Liv nodded. "I'll be right there," she said. "I want to check around here again."

Jen went back downstairs and turned the stove off, then drained the pasta. She put some on a plate for herself, then added sauce and sprinkled cheese on top. She took her plate to the table, then brought the bowl of salad over. She waited for Aunt Liv to come down, but after a few minutes she decided to start eating before the spaghetti got cold.

She was almost done when Liv finally appeared in the kitchen. Liv got herself some pasta and sat down. She twirled it around with her fork but didn't eat any. Jen wished she would say something—anything—to break the silence. She had no idea how to help. Worse, she was afraid that her aunt blamed her for the missing doll head.

"How was your trip?" Jen finally asked.

"Unproductive," Aunt Liv said, still twirling her spaghetti without picking any up. Then she sighed. "Sorry," she said. "It's been a long day. And then I came home and found the doll head missing. I'm just not in a great mood. Tell me about *your* day. What did you and Joe do?"

"He took me to meet Edith," Jen said.

"I'm sure that was interesting," Aunt Liv said. "Did she tell you about the spacemen?"

Jen shook her head. "Mermaids," she said.

"Of course," said Liv. "You have to be very careful about the mermaids, you know."

"What do you think she's really hearing?" she asked her aunt. "She said they've been really loud."

"Seals, maybe," said Liv. "Loons calling to one another. I don't know. But I love that she makes up these fantastic stories about it. Edith has a wild imagination."

Jen didn't mention the little jar of ghost powder, which was sitting on the dresser in the Yellow Room. She wasn't sure why she didn't tell Aunt Liv about it. She didn't think her aunt would be upset about it or anything. But she decided to keep that story to herself for now.

"Dinner is great," Liv told Jen, which was a funny thing to say given that she hadn't actually eaten any of it. "Thanks for making it. I'm going to go search the workroom again. Maybe I missed a spot."

She got up and left the kitchen. Jen finished her spaghetti and salad, then cleared the table and washed the dishes. When she was done, she went upstairs. As she passed the workroom, she heard Aunt Liv moving things around and talking to herself.

"Why would she take it?" she heard her aunt say. "I just don't understand."

She means me, Jen thought. *She still thinks I took the doll head.*

This made her feel awful. She wanted to go into the room and tell Aunt Liv that she hadn't taken it, and that she would never lie to her. But she couldn't. Her aunt obviously didn't believe her, or trust her, and nothing she could say would change that. She went up to the third floor and into the Yellow Room, where she shut the door and sat down on the bed. Tears threatened to flow, but she forced them back.

This is all Maddie's fault, she thought. But Aunt Liv seemed to have forgotten that Jen wasn't the only other person in the house the night before. She wanted to go remind her, but she also didn't want to give her aunt something else to be upset about.

She was sure Maddie had taken the head from Pearl's doll. It was the only thing that made sense. Maybe she was trying to make Jen look like a liar. Maybe she just wanted it. Or maybe it was part of Chester McKiser's plan somehow. Jen didn't know what Maddie's reason for taking the doll head was. But she was absolutely certain Maddie had it.

She tried to distract herself by reading, but she kept skimming the same page over and over without remembering anything about the story. She set the book down and went to the window. Outside, birds and insects were chirping in the darkness. Was that what Edith heard when she thought the mermaids were singing? It didn't really sound like words.

She just has an overactive imagination, Jen thought.

She went to the dresser and picked up the jar of ghost repellent. Edith really seemed to believe it was magical, but it was just dirt and salt and who knew what else mixed together. It couldn't actually *do* anything. Especially since ghosts weren't real.

Jen unscrewed the lid on the jar and poured some of the powder into her hand. It didn't look like anything special. She sniffed it. It didn't smell like anything special. She wasn't about to taste it, but she was sure it didn't taste like anything special either.

She went over to the doorway. Taking a pinch of the powder between her fingers, she sprinkled it lightly along the bottom of her door. It made a faint line on the wood floor. She put the lid back on the jar, then returned it to the top of the dresser. She didn't know why she had done it. It was silly. But Edith had gone through the trouble of making the powder for her, so she felt like she should at least pretend it was real.

She got into bed and lay there, staring at the ceiling, her mind swirling with unhappy thoughts. She imagined Aunt Liv searching for the missing doll head and was still thinking about this when she finally fell into a restless sleep.

Her brain turned her worries into a dream in which she

was looking through a room for the doll head. The room was filled with lots of pieces of paper and scraps of fabric, all of which could easily hide a doll head. In her dream, Jen searched through it. She kept thinking maybe she saw the doll under something, but every time she lifted up the paper or fabric, there was nothing there.

Aunt Liv was also in the dream. She too was searching for the doll head. And she kept saying, over and over, "Why would she take it? I just don't understand." Jen tried to say "I didn't take it!" but her voice wouldn't come out.

All of a sudden, thunder shook the house and a gust of wind came out of nowhere to whip the pieces of paper and fabric into a swirling tornado of scraps that filled the room. Jen couldn't see anything. She tried to bat the pieces of cloth and paper away, but they fluttered all around her head like moths.

"My daddy is over the ocean."

The voice rose out of the storm, thin and eerie.

"My daddy is over the sea."

Jen thought about Edith and the mermaids. Was this the song she heard them singing?

"My daddy is over the ocean."

Jen tossed and turned in her sleep, trying to speak. Finally, her throat unlocked. "Pearl?" she called out. "Is that you?"

"Please bring back my daddy to me."

A crack of lightning shook the house and Jen woke up. The door to her room was open. The hallway was filled with a sickly greenish-yellow light as if the house was some- how underwater. Strange shapes darted along the walls. And standing just outside the door, looking into the room, was the ghostly form of a girl.

"Pearl," Jen whispered.

She looked exactly like she did in the painting in the Pink Room. Only she was transparent, flickering in and out. She was looking down at the floor, and Jen realized that she was touching the line of Edith's powder with her toe, and that every time she did, her form crackled.

She really can't cross it, Jen thought.

Pearl looked up at her. She looked angry. Jen's heart beat faster. What was Pearl going to do? Would the powder really stop her from coming into the room?

Pearl reached out with one hand, palm up. As it started to pass through the doorway, it suddenly stopped and the crackling happened again. Pearl pressed harder, and the light around her hand bent and sparked as if she was touching something solid. Her face contorted in anger as she let out a ragged moan and pulled her hand back.

No, Jen realized. *She's not angry. That hurt her. She's afraid now. And sad.*

Then Jen saw that Pearl was holding something in her other hand. It was the doll head. Pearl was cradling it to her chest.

"Please bring back my daddy to me," Pearl sang, her voice plaintive as she stood looking at Jen.

"I don't know how," Jen told her.

"Please bring back my daddy to me," Pearl said again. "Please."

As she uttered the last word, she tried once more to step into the room. When she did, her body seemed to break up into thousands of sparks of light, and she vanished with a strangled cry of despair. The doorway was empty. Jen waited for her to return, but nothing happened.

Pearl was gone.

12

The next morning, Jen met the ferry at the dock.

"Is there a hardware store on the mainland?" she asked Joe when he got off.

"Two of them," he said. "Why?"

"I have an idea," Jen said without giving further details. "Can I ride back with you?"

"Sure," said Joe. "But you have to tell me what's up. That's the fare."

On the way over, Jen told him her plan.

"You want to catch a ghost on camera?" Joe said when she finished explaining what had happened the night before, and what she was planning to do next.

"Yep," said Jen. "My parents use trail cameras all the time to get footage of animals. I bet I can do the same thing with Pearl's ghost."

"So now you believe in ghosts?" Joe teased.

"I don't know," said Jen. "I saw *something*. And it sure looked like Pearl. But I know if I was Aunt Liv I wouldn't believe me, so I want to get proof before I say anything."

"You think Pearl really took her doll's head?"

"It's not anywhere in the house," Jen said. "And she was holding it in her hand last night."

"What if you just dreamed it all?" Joe said. "I've had some dreams that definitely felt real."

"Now it sounds like you're the one who doesn't believe in ghosts," said Jen.

"Let's see what the camera catches," Joe told her.

Jen didn't blame Joe for being skeptical. She still wasn't totally convinced that she'd seen a ghost either. Even though it had all felt very real, part of her still thought she'd made it all up. If she could capture Pearl's ghost on camera, though, it would prove to her—and everyone else—that she wasn't just telling a creepy story.

When the ferry docked, she and Joe got off and walked the short distance into town. There were a lot of places that Jen wished she could go into, but she had a mission to complete and focused on finding a trail camera. The first hardware store they went into didn't have any, but the second one did. It took a big chunk of the money her parents had given her for emergencies to buy it, but Jen figured this was absolutely an emergency.

After the hardware store, there was time before the next ferry trip back to Big Rock Island, so Jen and Joe stopped at the used bookstore and browsed for a while. Then they made one final stop, at a bakery, where Jen bought half a dozen fancy cupcakes. She thought they might cheer Aunt Liv up. Then, while they waited for the ferry, she checked the messages on her phone and discovered her parents had sent her some great photos of spiders in Costa Rica. She sent them back a message telling them she missed them and that her visit was going great. She wished she could tell them everything that was going on, but it would take too long to explain and would only make them worry.

Once the ferry was back at Big Rock Island, Jen walked quickly to Pratchett House. She left the box of cupcakes on the kitchen counter and went upstairs. Aunt Liv had given up looking for the missing doll head and was working on a different doll, and she didn't even turn around as Jen walked by. Jen was relieved, since she hadn't told her she was going to the mainland, only saying she was going to explore the island some more. Now she wondered if Aunt Liv had even noticed she was gone all morning.

Back in the Yellow Room, she unboxed the trail camera. Usually, it would get mounted to a tree or something else near where animals passed by or stopped. This one also came with a little tripod, which Jen attached to the camera. She set the camera up on the floor so that it focused on her doorway and the hallway beyond it. Then she turned it on and did a test run, walking up and down the hallway and stopping in her doorway. When she checked the camera, it had recorded everything. She could see herself clearly.

Now I need you to catch Pearl, she thought as she reset the camera.

How she was going to get Pearl to appear was the problem. The powder Edith had given her did exactly the opposite. It kept her away. Jen wanted her to show up. She needed to figure out how—or if—she could make that happen.

The first thing was to make sure there was no anti-ghost powder left in the doorway. She got a washcloth from the bathroom, wet it, and wiped up every speck of dust she could find. If Pearl wanted to go in the Yellow Room, now there was nothing stopping her. But Jen needed to do more than that. She had to make sure Pearl would come in. She just didn't know how to do that.

I bet Edith would know, she thought. This was probably true. But Edith was the one who'd told her she needed to watch out for ghosts and gave her the anti-ghost powder in the first place. She wasn't likely to tell Jen how to get a ghost to appear. She had to think of something else.

Then she remembered the music box. The first time something weird had happened, the music box had been playing. Maybe if she played it she could get Pearl to appear. She went to the Pink Room and got it, bringing it back to the Yellow Room.

Now she had another problem. If she played the music box, Aunt Liv would hear it and ask her what she was doing. She couldn't very well say that she was trying to summon the ghost of Pearl Pratchett. Aunt Liv already seemed to think she wasn't trustworthy. Jen didn't need her thinking she had lost her mind too.

For the rest of the afternoon, she tried to think of a way to play the music box without Aunt Liv hearing it. But even after doing the dishes, she still hadn't thought of anything. Then Aunt Liv solved the problem for her.

"I'm going to do some work in the basement," she

announced. "I need to make some more doll stands for a special order. You won't be able to hear the saws on the third floor, though, so it shouldn't bother you."

"Okay," Jen said, trying not to sound too excited. If Aunt Liv was downstairs running the power tools, there was no way she would hear the music box playing.

As soon as Liv went downstairs and closed the door, Jen raced up to the third floor. It was barely dark outside, and Jen hoped that was enough. She didn't know why, really, but she thought ghosts probably only came out at night. Anyway, the weird things happening in Pratchett House only happened at night.

After making sure the trail camera was on, she turned out the lights in the Yellow Room. Then she wound the music box, set it on the floor, and opened the lid. Immediately it began playing "My Bonnie Lies over the Ocean."

Come on, Pearl, she thought as she sat on the edge of the bed, waiting.

The music box continued to play for what felt like

forever. Nothing happened. The box slowed, then stopped playing at all. Jen picked it up and wound it again. She was really tired of hearing "My Bonnie Lies over the Ocean." Now the song was stuck in her head, though, and she found herself singing along to it. Only she sang the words like Pearl did.

"My daddy is over the ocean," she sang. "My daddy is over the sea. My daddy is over the ocean."

"Please bring back my daddy to me."

That wasn't just me, Jen thought.

Another voice was singing with her. She began the song again. This time, she was singing a duet.

"My daddy is over the ocean," their voices sang together.

The air in the hallway shimmered. The greenish-yellow light seeped up through the floor and started to climb the walls, as if Pratchett House was falling into the sea.

"My daddy is over the sea," Jen sang, her heart pounding.

The shimmering in the hallway grew brighter. Large

figures swam along the walls, flicking their fishlike tails and vanishing before Jen could tell if they were mermaids or something else. Then Pearl Pratchett appeared. She was clutching the head of her doll.

"My daddy is over the ocean," she sang on her own. "Please bring back my daddy to me."

Jen glanced at the trail cam. The little red light that indicated it was recording was blinking in the darkness. It was working!

Jen heard the music box begin to slow. The ghost of Pearl Pratchett seemed to dim as it did. Jen picked the box up and wound it again. She wanted to get as much footage of Pearl as she could.

The hallway behind Pearl lit up as the lights went on. Pearl vanished.

"Is everything okay up here?" Aunt Liv asked. "Was that the music box I heard?"

"Yes," Jen said excitedly. "I was, um, trying something. And it worked!"

Aunt Liv looked at her with a puzzled expression.

Jen snatched up the trail camera. "I know who took the doll head. Here, I'll show you."

"What is that?" Aunt Liv asked as she came into the room.

"Proof!" Jen said. "Just watch."

She hit the PLAY button on the camera. The recorded video started to play. Jen couldn't wait for Aunt Liv to see what was on it.

Then she saw herself appear on the screen. She was standing in the doorway of the Yellow Room. And she was holding the missing doll head.

13

Jen played the recording back again.

Again, she saw herself standing in the doorway of the Yellow Room holding the doll head and grinning at the camera. Aunt Liv saw it too.

"I don't understand," Jen said. "It was Pearl."

Aunt Liv sighed. "Jen, it's okay. I know you miss your parents. And it's hard being in a strange place."

"But it wasn't me!" Jen insisted. "Pearl really was there. I saw her. She was holding the doll head."

"The only thing I see on that recording is you," said Liv.

"It isn't me!" Jen cried. "I mean, it is me on that

recording. But it wasn't me standing there. It was Pearl."

Aunt Liv didn't say anything, which was worse than if she *had* said something. Jen knew she didn't believe the story about Pearl having been there. And she didn't blame her aunt. All the evidence said that Jen was making up the story.

"If it was me, then where's the doll head?" she said. "It should be here, right?"

"Good question," said Aunt Liv. "Yes, it should be." She looked at Jen with a questioning expression.

"I don't have it!" Jen said. "Pearl does!"

"Jen," Aunt Liv said. "We're both upset. I'm going to go back to what I was working on. I think you should get to bed. Maybe later you can find the doll head and put it back where it belongs, okay?"

Jen didn't say anything. Anything she did say would either make things worse or be a lie. She couldn't find the doll head because she had no idea where it was, so she couldn't promise Aunt Liv that it would be back on the workbench. She sat on the bed, staring at the screen on the trail cam.

"Okay," Aunt Liv said. "We'll talk later."

She left the Yellow Room. Jen hit the PLAY button on the trail cam. The screen crackled with static. Then the image of Pearl Pratchett appeared, looking straight out at Jen. She was holding the doll head.

"Aunt Liv!" Jen called out as she scrambled to her feet and ran into the hallway. "Wait!"

Liv turned around. Jen hit PLAY again. But instead of Pearl, it was herself she saw. Her heart sank.

"What is it?" Aunt Liv asked.

Jen shook her head. "Nothing," she said. "I just wanted to say sorry."

Aunt Liv nodded. "Okay," she said. "Good night."

Jen wanted to cry as she watched her aunt walk away. Why was Pearl doing this to her? Didn't she want Aunt Liv to know she was there? Frustration welled up in Jen like a balloon threatening to burst. She had no idea what to do to fix the mess she'd made. *That Pearl made*, she reminded herself.

She needed to get out of Pratchett House. Being in there

felt like being caught in a trap. She tossed the trail cam onto the bed in the Yellow Room, put on her sneakers, and walked downstairs. The door to Aunt Liv's workroom was closed, so Jen was able to get outside without anyone seeing her but a Nix who was sitting on the front porch.

"I'm just going for a walk," Jen told the Nix, who blinked pale green eyes and meowed as if to say "Be careful."

It was dark now, but the waxing moon overhead was more than bright enough for Jen to see by. Besides, she knew the road around the island well by now and walked without even thinking about it. Anyway, there was too much going on in her head for her to be worried about the direction she was going in. She just wanted to walk.

At the fork, she went left, and soon found herself approaching the old lighthouse. The moon seemed to be hanging above it like a spotlight, and the whole top of the bluff was bathed in a silvery glow. The lighthouse tower rose up against the sky, shadowlike, and the windows at the top sparkled.

Jen was drawn to the edge of the cliff. She stood there, looking out at the sea. It too gleamed beneath the moonlight. It also seemed rougher than usual, as if something under the surface was stirring.

"Can you hear them?" a voice said.

Jen, startled, whirled around. Standing behind her, about twenty feet away, was a man. At first she thought it was Chester McKiser, and that he was going to scold her for being at the lighthouse. But then she saw the man had a long beard. He was also wearing a heavy coat, which seemed weird in the warm summer air.

"Hear who?" Jen asked. She felt like she ought to be afraid that a strange man was standing behind her, but for some reason she wasn't.

"The sirens," the man said.

"Sirens?" said Jen. "I don't hear any sirens." She assumed the man meant something like a fire alarm or police car.

"Must be yer not a sailor," the man said. "Their song is for seafarin' men. Be glad you don't. Nothin' good will come of it."

Jen still didn't understand what the man was talking about. Then she remembered what Edith had said. "Do you mean mermaids?" she asked.

"Aye," the man said. "Something like."

His voice sounded funny, both because of a thick accent and because he was drawing his words out slowly, as if it was hard to talk.

Like he's been drinking, Jen thought. He was talking like drunk people in movies did.

"Storm will be here soon," the man said. "Should be lightin' the light."

Jen was confused. According to Joe, the lighthouse hadn't been used in years. Anyone living on the island would know that. Then, like pieces of a puzzle falling into place, she thought she might know who the man was.

"Arthur?" she said.

The man turned to look at her. "You know me," he said. "But I don't know you. Who might you be?"

Jen tried not to think about the fact that she was talking

to someone who had died hundreds of years earlier. "My name is Jen," she said. "My aunt lives in Pratchett House."

"Pratchett House?" Arthur said. "That's where William and Pearl live."

"They did," Jen said. "But they're . . ." She didn't finish the sentence.

"Should be lightin' the light," Arthur said again. "Sirens are singin'. Storm will be here soon." He turned and started walking toward the lighthouse. His steps were uneven, and he staggered and almost fell. He stopped, standing in place and swaying back and forth.

Jen didn't know what to do. Could she help Arthur? She had no idea how. The whole thing felt like a dream anyway. Maybe she was imagining all of it.

Suddenly, the moonlight dimmed as clouds rolled across the moon. The wind picked up, teasing Jen's hair and blowing it around her face. When she brushed it away, Arthur was gone. She was alone on the bluff, looking at the lighthouse.

She waited for Arthur to reappear. He didn't. The wind grew stronger, coming in from the ocean, and Jen shivered as the air around her grew colder. It began to rain, gently at first and then harder. The drops pelted Jen's skin.

She turned and looked up. Thick clouds now covered the moon, making it hard to see. It was as if something dark had wrapped the bluff in shadows. The rain fell harder and the wind increased. Through it, Jen thought she heard the sound of voices.

The sirens, she thought. *They're singing. Just like Arthur said.*

She tried to make out words but couldn't. What she heard could just be the sound of the wind and the ocean, or birds calling in the night. Maybe it was seals barking. Or the foxes Joe had shown her in the woods.

Or maybe it's not, she thought.

Thunder broke overhead, laughing at her. She knew that standing on the cliff edge in a storm wasn't a smart thing to do. Especially if the ghost of a long-dead lighthouse keeper might be hanging around. Although Arthur Crunk hadn't been at all threatening, Jen was quickly developing a mistrust of ghosts, given the prank Pearl Pratchett had pulled on her earlier.

She walked away, passing the lighthouse. She looked up at it and saw something glowing softly in the windowed room where the light was. Was it Arthur, trying to get the light going again? Or was it just a stray bit of moonlight? The rain streamed down, covering her eyes and making it impossible to see anything.

Jen ducked her head and walked as quickly as she could toward Pratchett House. Her feet squelched in her wet sneakers, and she was soon soaked through. When she reached her aunt's house, she was greeted by three Nixes huddled on the porch, watching the rain fall down. She took her shoes off, left them on the porch to dry, and went inside.

She found a dish towel in the kitchen and used it to pat off as much of the rain as she could. Then she went into the living room and over to a bookcase. The portrait of Captain Pratchett was above it. It showed him standing with his hand resting on an ornately carved chest. He regarded Jen with a stern look.

Jen scanned the rows of books, looking for one she remembered seeing there a few days earlier. She found it and took it with her as she went upstairs to the Yellow Room, where she shut the door. She got out of her wet clothes and into some dry ones, then sat on the bed and picked up the book. It was called *The Encyclopedia of Imaginary Things*.

Turning to the index, Jen ran her finger down the list of entries until she found one for sirens, then turned to the page number she found next to it.

"Now often confused with mermaids, sirens were originally creatures that had the bodies of birds and the heads of women," Jen read. "They sang beautiful songs designed to lure sailors to their deaths."

So, Arthur and Edith were talking about the same creatures. They were just using different names for them. That solved one part of the mystery. But it was a very small part.

Jen still didn't understand why Pearl had taken the doll head and then made it look like she had done it herself. Did she want something? What?

Jen felt like she was supposed to help somehow. But she needed more information. Unfortunately, she feared the only two people who could give her that information were ghosts. And she didn't know how to talk to ghosts.

She thought she knew someone who might, though.

14

The rain was still falling the next morning when Jen made the walk to Edith's house on the point. This time, she wore a rain jacket and brought an umbrella, so that when she got there she wasn't *quite* as wet as she'd been the night before.

She'd wanted to ask Joe to come with her, but because of the storm the ferry was delayed, so she'd decided to go herself. Now that she was standing at Edith's front door, though, she wondered if she'd made a mistake. Before she could convince herself that she had, she knocked three times.

Edith didn't answer right away, and Jen was just about to

turn around and leave when the door opened. When Edith saw her, she said, "Did the powder work?"

"Um, yes," Jen said. "But I have some more ghost problems. I was hoping you might be able to help."

"That's usually how it is with ghosts," Edith said, nodding. "Come in."

Jen went inside, setting her umbrella beside the door and removing her jacket, which Edith took and hung on a hook. Then they went into the kitchen, where there were already two mugs sitting on the table.

"I had a feeling someone would be coming," Edith said. "Made some tea."

Jen sat down and picked the mug up. It was wonderfully warm and took some of the chill out of her hands. The steam rising from it smelled like oranges and cinnamon. Edith sat down across from her. "Tell me about the ghost."

"Ghosts," Jen said. "There are two now."

Edith clucked her tongue and lifted an eyebrow. "Are there now?"

Jen nodded. "You were right about Pearl Pratchett coming back for the doll head," she said. "And last night I saw Arthur Crunk at the lighthouse."

"Poor Arthur," Edith said. "He must have heard the mermaids."

"He called them sirens," Jen told her. "And yes, he did."

Edith was looking at Jen with an interested expression. "You don't sound like you're afraid," she said. "Most people would be."

Jen thought about this for a moment. "I'm not," she said, realizing it was true. "I feel a lot of things, but not afraid. I don't really know why, but I'm not. I think they want my help."

"I think they do too," Edith said.

"Do you know what they want?" Jen asked.

Edith shook her head. "It's got something to do with the doll," she said. "That's all I know. But we can ask."

This was exactly what Jen had been hoping Edith would say. "How?"

"There are lots of ways to talk to spirits," Edith said. "But I think we should use the treasure box."

As Jen wondered what the treasure box was, Edith got up and went into the other room. When she came back she was carrying a shoebox-sized wooden box, which she set on the table.

"How does it work?" Jen asked.

Edith lifted the lid off the box and set it aside. Jen peered into the box. It was filled with all kinds of small objects. Some were plastic or ceramic animals. Others were miniature things you might find in a doll's house. Then there were things like stones and fishhooks and buttons.

"I've found that sometimes it's easier for those who have passed on to communicate ideas rather than actual words," Edith said. "It's like they have memories, but the memories have faded and they can't quite tell you what they want. But they can show you. Sometimes. Sort of." She laughed. "Ghosts!" she said, as if this explained everything.

"How does it work?" Jen asked.

"You ask the spirit to guide your hand," Edith said. "Then you reach in and pick several objects without looking at them. The things you pick will—well, might—give you an idea of what the spirit wants to tell you."

"You mean I have to pick the things out of the box?" Jen said.

"In this case, with Pearl's help," said Edith. "Since you're the one she's appeared to, you have the closest connection to her."

Jen looked at the box. She wasn't at all convinced this would work, but she was willing to give it a try. "Okay," she said. "What do I do?"

"Ask Pearl to tell you what she wants you to know," Edith said. "Then start picking."

"That's it?" Jen said. "We don't have to say anything special? Or sprinkle some powder around?"

Edith laughed. "Sometimes all you have to do is ask," she said.

Jen took a deep breath and thought about what she

wanted to say. "Hey, Pearl," she began. "I don't know what you want, but I'd like to help you. Can you tell me why you're here?"

She looked at Edith, who nodded. "Select the first item," she said.

Jen reached into the box and let her fingers feel around. She tried not to think about what the items she was touching were and to just choose something that felt right. But how would she know? Should she just take out the first thing she grabbed? What if she jabbed herself on a fishhook?

She was thinking all these thoughts when she got what felt like a little shock. She gasped as her fingertips tingled.

"That's it!" Edith whispered. "You've found one."

Jen picked up the thing she was touching and took it out. It was a doll's head, plastic, complete with short blonde hair. Jen set it down on the tabletop.

"Well, that makes sense," she said.

"Keep going," Edith urged.

Jen put her hand back in the box. Again, she tried not to

think about what she was doing. Instead, she kept her attention on the doll head on the table. It stared back with painted eyes.

Again, Jen felt a little jolt of some kind of energy. Again, she picked up the object she was touching when it happened. This time she removed a small ceramic arm from the box. She laid it beside the head.

"Another doll part," she said as she put her hand back into the box.

This time the zap happened almost immediately. It was so strong that Jen actually gave a little yelp of surprise. When she removed the object that had caused it, she was holding an old-fashioned metal key.

"Should I keep going?" she asked Edith, who nodded.

Jen reached back into the box, half expecting her hand to begin tingling right away. But this time, nothing happened. She let her fingertips drift over the collection of objects inside the treasure chest, but after several minutes she hadn't felt anything at all.

"I think she's done," Edith said.

Jen took her hand out. She looked at the three items she'd selected from the box and tried to put together a message from them. The doll's head was obviously about the doll's head she'd found and that Pearl had then taken. But what about the other two things?

"This arm could represent the rest of the doll," Jen suggested.

"Very good," said Edith. "And the key?"

"Well, maybe it's literally a key?" said Jen. "As in the key to solving the mystery." She sighed. "That's not exactly helpful, though."

Edith snorted. "I told you, sometimes the spirits only know so much," she said. "Even about their own needs. The important thing is that Pearl seems to believe you can help her."

"Great," Jen said. "I wish I believed it too."

"I said to you before that I think finding the body of the doll will answer some of your questions," Edith said. "I'd say Pearl has confirmed this."

"I wish she would tell us where it is," Jen said.

"She probably doesn't know any more than you do," said Edith.

Jen was frustrated. It was great—and weird—that communicating with Pearl through the treasure box seemed to have worked. But there was a lot she still didn't know. Like what to do next.

She was about to thank Edith for her help when her hand started tingling. And not just in her fingertips. Her whole hand was buzzing from the inside. She'd once gotten a shock from an electrical wire, and that's what it felt like.

"I think Pearl wants me to get something else out of the box," she said.

Edith pointed at the treasure chest. "Go ahead."

Jen reached into the chest. Immediately, the tingling in her hand grew more intense. She started touching things, feeling the sensation grow weaker or stronger as she moved around. Then, while touching something, her fingers lit up like sparklers. She grabbed the item that was producing the reaction and took it out.

She was holding a miniature book. The title on it was familiar to her—*The Shining*. It was by Stephen King. It was the book Maddie had been reading when Jen first met her sitting on the rock at the beach.

"How odd," Edith said. "I made that for a miniature display at the library. I wonder how it got in there. I don't remember putting it in the box. Does it mean something to you?"

"Unfortunately, yes," Jen answered.

The message of Pearl's final clue was clear—she was going to have to ask Maddie for help.

15

"I know what you're doing."

Maddie stared at Jen, who was standing on the porch while rain poured down. "Um, what am I doing?"

"Working for Chester McKiser," Jen said. "I know all about it."

"No, you don't," said Maddie.

Jen was confused. She thought Maddie would deny everything, but it sounded like she was confessing. That made no sense. "I don't?" she said.

"Come in," said Maddie. "You're getting soaked."

Jen went into the house.

"Take your stuff off," Maddie said. "I'll get you a towel."

While Maddie went into the bathroom, Jen took off her jacket and sneakers. Maddie came back and handed her a towel, which Jen used to dry off. Maddie took the towel back and returned it to the bathroom while Jen took a seat on the couch.

"Okay," Maddie said when she got back. "What is it you think you know?"

"I heard you and Chester talking," Jen said. "In the lighthouse. When he said he would pay you to pretend to be my friend."

"What were you doing in the lighthouse?"

"I wanted to see it," Jen said. "And I was looking for clues."

"Clues to what?"

"There's been a lot of weird stuff going on at Pratchett House," Jen told her. "I asked Joe to help me look around the lighthouse. We were in the tower when you and your uncle came in."

"Joe knows about this too?" Maddie said.

Jen nodded.

Maddie sat down on a chair across from Jen. "I know what you heard sounded bad," she said.

"You mean the part where you agreed to work for Chester to help get my aunt's house?" Jen said. "Yeah, that sounded pretty bad."

"That's what you get for listening to other people's conversations," Maddie said.

This made Jen mad. "You're the one who pretended you wanted to be my friend!"

Maddie nodded. "Yeah," she said. "I did. At first."

"What do you mean at first?" said Jen.

"Ugh," Maddie said. "Don't make me say it."

"Say what?"

"That I actually kind of like you," said Maddie. She made a face, as if she'd just eaten something really sour.

"Really?" Jen said. "You weren't just pretending?"

"Like I said, at first I was," Maddie answered. "But only at first. I'm not used to having friends, okay?"

Hearing this made Jen happy. Then she remembered why she was there. "But you were still sneaking around my aunt's house," she said. "I saw you."

"Do you always spy on people?" Maddie asked.

"I was getting a cookie," Jen said. "And stop changing the subject. What were you looking for? And why are you still helping Chester?"

"I was getting to that," Maddie said. "I'm not helping Chester. He just thinks I am."

"Then what *are* you doing?" Jen said. "Because it sure looks like you're helping him."

"I'm collecting evidence against him," Maddie explained. "You know how he's trying to basically turn Big Rock Island into his personal hotel?"

Jen nodded.

"Well, I don't like that. A lot of people don't like that. I mean, yeah, he's my uncle. But he's nothing like Little Tom. Sometimes I wonder if they're even really related. Anyway, I thought I could expose him once and for all as only being out to make money for himself."

"Oh," Jen said. "That actually kind of makes sense."

"I even recorded our conversation," Maddie said. She reached into the pocket of the hoodie she was wearing and took out a tiny device. She hit a button and Jen heard Chester's voice.

"That's the conversation I heard in the lighthouse," Jen said.

"I got the whole thing," said Maddie.

"Then you didn't really need to actually do what he asked you to," Jen said.

"Technically, no," Maddie agreed. "But I thought getting more evidence was a good idea. Also, I was kind of curious about why he wanted me to get into Pratchett House."

"What did he want?" Jen was curious about that too.

"That's where it got interesting," Maddie said. "Once I got you to invite me over, he asked me to check out the cellar."

"That's weird," Jen said. "I mean, it's just a cellar."

"He's looking for something," Maddie said. "But he wouldn't say what. He just wanted me to look in the cellar for places where someone might hide something. We're supposed to meet today so he can tell me what he wants me to do next."

"Where are you supposed to meet him?"

"At the lighthouse again. He's coming over on the afternoon ferry. I'm hoping he'll tell me exactly what it is he's looking for or trying to do. Then I can expose him once and for all."

Jen ran over everything Maddie had just told her. There was a lot to think about. But first there was something she needed to do. "I'm sorry," she told Maddie. "For thinking you were up to something."

Maddie snorted. "I *am* up to something," she said. "Just not what you thought I was up to."

"Chester McKiser really is a jerk," Jen said. Then she sighed. "But he's not the biggest problem."

Now it was Maddie's turn to look confused. "What do you mean?"

Jen told her about the letter from the bank. "And that's not all," she said.

"You mean it gets worse?" Maddie said. "How can it get worse?"

Jen told her about seeing the ghosts of Pearl Pratchett and Arthur Crunk. Then about going to Edith's house that morning and picking the little book out of the box. "I know this all sounds totally wild," she concluded.

"It does," Maddie said.

Jen frowned. "You don't believe me."

"Oh, I believe you," Maddie said.

Jen looked at her, surprised. "Really?"

"You've seen the books I read," Maddie said. "Compared to those stories, this is nothing. A couple of ghosts? Killer clowns and werewolves I might need more proof to believe in, but ghosts make sense."

For a second Jen thought Maddie might be making fun of her. Then Maddie said, "We need to figure out where the rest of Pearl's doll is."

"That's what I think too," Jen said. "I just don't know why."

"Usually, when ghosts come back it's because they have unfinished business," Maddie said. "At least in all the stories I've read that's usually why they're around. They can't move on until something or other is found or they take care of something left undone when they died."

Jen liked the way Maddie talked about ghosts as if they were something people dealt with all the time. It made the situation feel slightly less creepy. But only a little. She still couldn't believe they were actually discussing ghosts and how to help them.

"People say Arthur hangs around because he feels responsible for what happened," she said, trying to work through the problem. "We can't do anything to change history, though."

"Right," Maddie said. "But we might be able to help Pearl find her missing doll. For some reason, that's really important to her."

"It could be anywhere," said Jen. "The head was on the bottom of the ocean. What if the rest of the doll is too? We'll never find it."

The two of them sat in silence, thinking. No ideas were coming to Jen, and from the look on Maddie's face, Jen knew she wasn't having any luck either. They needed another clue.

The front door opened, and Little Tom came in. "There you are," he said, and Jen realized he was speaking to her. "Liv was looking for you."

"I should get home then," Jen said, standing up.

"No need," Little Tom said. "She wanted to tell you she had to go to the mainland. Although I suspect she's going to regret that."

"Why?" Jen asked.

"Storm is coming in fast," Little Tom said. "My guess is the ferry won't be coming back today."

"What will she do?" said Jen, worried now.

"Oh, she's got friends she can stay with over there," Little

Tom said. "She'll be okay. And your friend Joe is stuck on this end, by the way."

"We should go find him," Maddie said. "You know, to make sure he's all right."

Little Tom laughed. "He actually seemed pretty excited about the idea of spending the night on Big Rock," he said.

"Still," Maddie said, motioning for Jen to come with her. "We'll go check on him."

"Be careful," Little Tom said. "It's coming down out there. Stay away from the beach and the rocks."

"Will do," Maddie said as she pulled a rain jacket on and Jen got back into her gear.

A minute later they were walking toward town. The rain was falling harder than it had been earlier.

"Where are we going?" Jen asked Maddie.

"To Soco's," Maddie said. "We're going to get Joe. Then we're going to your aunt's house to figure out what to do next."

"You think Joe will be able to help?" Jen said.

"He knows this island better than anyone else I can think of," Maddie said. "If there's a place for a doll body to be hidden, he can find it."

Jen hoped Maddie was right. The storm felt like a warning. Like time was running out to solve the mystery.

A crack of lightning split the sky. The rain fell harder. It was like even the weather was telling them to hurry.

Before it was too late.

16

"How can you eat pancakes right now?"

Jen looked at Joe, who was seated at the counter at Soco's. She and Maddie had just finished telling him about what was going on. Joe stuck his fork into a pancake and waved it at her. "How can you not?" he asked.

Jen and Maddie waited for him to finish and clear his dishes away. Then he came back to the counter. "So," he said. "Ghosts."

"Yes," Maddie said, sounding exasperated. "Ghosts. Two of them."

"That's really cool," Joe said. "And you think Pearl needs us to help her find the body of her doll?"

"Right," Jen said. "So, do you have any ideas where we might look?"

Joe scratched his head. "About a million different places," he said.

Jen groaned. This was exactly what she'd been afraid he would say.

"But I think we should start at the lighthouse," Joe said.

"The lighthouse?" said Maddie. "Why there?"

"Because it's the last place a ghost appeared," Joe said. "Maybe Arthur will show up again and we can ask him some more questions."

"Why not go back to Pratchett House and see if Pearl shows up so we can ask her?" said Jen.

"Because we already know she doesn't know where the doll is," Joe said.

Maddie looked at Jen. "I hate to admit he's right, but it does make sense."

"It's the pancakes," Joe said. "They help me think. All the antioxidants or whatever in the blueberries. Let's go."

The three of them left Soco's and headed for the lighthouse. Even though it was still early, the heavy clouds and driving rain made it feel much later. It was hard to see more than a little way ahead, and nobody felt like talking since the rain was doing its best to completely soak them. By the time they reached the top of the hill, the trio was bedraggled and muddy.

The door to the lighthouse was still unlocked, and they went inside. It wasn't any warmer in there, and Jen felt herself shiver from being soaked through. But it was more than that. Something about the lighthouse felt not right, as if a heavy sadness had settled over it along with the rain clouds.

"Someone's here," Maddie said. She pointed to the floor, where wet footprints disappeared into the other room.

"Yes," a voice said. "Somebody is."

Chester McKiser emerged from the shadows beyond the doorway and came into the room. He was wearing a dark raincoat that had helped hide him from view. He was also carrying something. A doll. A doll without a head.

"Is that—" Jen began, then cut herself off.

"Pearl Pratchett's doll?" Chester said. "I see you've figured that part of the mystery out."

"Where did you get it?" asked Maddie.

"Not that it's any of your business, but I bought it," Chester answered. "At an estate sale held by the family of the nurse who attended to Pearl Pratchett all those years ago. She apparently took the doll away with her and was going to have it repaired. She never did, but it stayed in the family. I went to the sale to look at an antique desk, and when they found out that I own property on Big Rock Island, they thought I would be interested in this. I could tell it was old, and thought it might be worth something, so I made them a ridiculously low offer and they accepted."

"It belongs to Pearl!" Jen said. "Give it back."

Chester laughed. "Pearl Pratchett died two hundred years ago," he said. "I don't think she's missing her doll."

"You might be surprised," Joe told him. "Anyway, what do you want with it? It's part of Big Rock Island history.

You should give it to Olivia so she can restore it."

"Big Rock Island history," Chester said, mimicking Joe's voice. "I'm so tired of hearing about the history of this god-forsaken place. That's all in the past. I'm looking to the future."

"Then why do you want an old doll?" Maddie said. "And why did you hire me to look around Pratchett House for you?"

"So many questions," Chester said. "I assume you told your friends here about our deal, so that's off, by the way. Anyway, from what I hear, Pratchett House will be on the market soon. I intend to buy it, so I don't need you anymore."

"Why would Olivia sell Pratchett House?" Maddie asked.

Chester looked at Jen. "You haven't told her?" he said. He laughed. "Jenny's aunt is experiencing some financial diffi-culties," he told Maddie. "She's behind on the mortgage. Of course, a word to my good friend who owns the bank that holds that mortgage might have sped up their decision to act on that."

"What!" Jen said. Rage filled her as Chester smirked at her.

"So, what was I looking for in there?" Maddie asked again.

Chester sighed. "I don't know," he said. As they watched, he reached into the body of the doll and pulled something out. He held it up for them to see.

"A key?" Jen said.

"I found it inside the body of the doll," Chester informed them. "It was wedged inside the hollow leg. At first, I assumed it got in there accidentally somehow. But it's engraved with the initials *WP*."

"William Pratchett," Jen said.

Chester nodded. "That's when I started to put things together. I started thinking—if I were a sea captain on a doomed ship and wanted to try and get a message to my beloved daughter on the island, what would I do?"

"Stick it inside a doll and toss it overboard," Maddie said.

"Smart girl," Chester said. "I knew you had a tricky

mind. Just like your uncle's. Yes, I would write a message and put it inside something that might float. And not just a plain old bottle. Something I knew my daughter would be looking for. Like the doll she was waiting for."

"You found a message?" Jen said. "Inside the doll?"

"No," said Chester, dropping the key back inside the doll body. "I assume that if there *was* one, it was long ago destroyed by the seawater when the head came off. I think the key is what's really important. If William Pratchett went to so much trouble to ensure his daughter received this key, it likely opens something of enormous value."

"Like what?" said Joe.

Chester held up a finger. "Aha! Now you're asking the correct question. Unfortunately, I don't have an answer. That's why I employed this budding criminal to help me find out."

"Hey!" Maddie said.

"I thought if I could get her inside Pratchett House, she could look around for me and we might discover what this key goes to," Chester continued.

"Why didn't you just tell me that?" said Maddie.

"I had to see if I could trust you first," said Chester. "Obviously, I can't. You're softhearted, like your father. Not that any of it matters now."

"Until I tell Aunt Olivia what you're up to," Jen said defiantly.

Chester laughed. "Tell her anything you want. By the time she's able to return to the island, she'll have received the news that Pratchett House has been foreclosed on."

Jen felt like charging at Chester McKiser and kicking him as hard as she could. She forced herself to stand still, though, and only *thought* about how good it would feel to do it.

Maddie, however, had a different plan. She ran at Chester, letting out a battle cry that startled him so much he couldn't even react before she reached him, snatched the doll out of his hands, and tossed it to Jen. "Run!" she shouted.

Jen caught the doll. She whirled around and ran out the front door and into the storm. Her feet slipped in the mud as she scrambled around, trying to decide where to go. She waited a moment too long, and suddenly Chester was coming out the door behind her.

"Give me that doll!" he shouted.

Running without thinking, Jen headed for the rear of the lighthouse. Only when she was dashing toward the end of the bluff did she realize she'd made a huge mistake. She stopped and turned around. Chester was coming right for her. Maddie and Joe were behind him. They both dived at him but missed, landing on their faces in the muddy grass.

Chester stopped not far from Jen. He grinned. "There's nowhere to go," he said.

Jen's mind raced as she tried to think of a way past Chester. Her friends were picking themselves up, but Chester had started coming toward her, his hands outstretched.

"Help!" Jen shouted into the wind and the rain.

She heard Chester laugh at her. Her heart raced as she waited to feel his hands grab her.

Suddenly, a silvery light flared up around her. She

glanced to her left and saw the ghost of Arthur Crunk standing beside her. Chester saw him too and stopped, his mouth hanging open in terror.

"Can you hear them?" Arthur said. "Can you hear them singin'?"

Jen stared at Chester. His whole demeanor had changed. He turned his head and looked past her, out to sea. Slowly, he nodded. Then, just as slowly, he began to walk toward the edge of the bluff. As he passed by Jen, she held her breath, but he didn't even look at her. He just kept going. It was like he was under some kind of enchantment.

Jen ran to where Maddie and Joe stood watching Chester walk away.

"What's he doing?" Joe asked.

"He hears the sirens," Jen said. "They're calling to him."

"He's going to walk right off the bluff," said Maddie.

Jen turned and looked. Chester stood on the very edge of the cliff, swaying slowly. The rain and wind surrounded him. The ghost of Arthur Crunk stood nearby. He looked at the three friends and nodded.

"We should go," Jen said.

The three of them started walking. Behind them, the wind howled a terrible song.

Jen didn't look back.

17

Jen flicked the light switch again. Nothing happened.

"The electricity is out," she said.

They were standing in the front room at Pratchett House. The storm surrounded them, making the interior of the house dark. Several Nixes, their tails twitching anxiously, darted in and out of the doorways like shadows.

"Aunt Olivia told me where the flashlights are in case this happened," Jen said, walking to the kitchen. She pulled open a cabinet and retrieved lights for each of them. When they were turned on, the house became a little brighter.

"Now what?" Joe said.

Jen turned the doll body she was carrying upside down. The key inside clattered onto the kitchen counter. Jen picked it up. "We figure out what this goes to," she said.

"It could be anything," said Maddie. "A door. A trunk. There must be a hundred different things it could open."

"Then we'll try them all," Joe said. "I say we start with doors."

Jen, who had been staring at the key and thinking hard, said, "No. I have another idea."

"Let's hear it," Maddie said.

"We'll ask Pearl," Jen answered.

"How are you going to get her to show up?" asked Joe.

"The same way I did last time," said Jen. "The music box. Come on."

She led the two of them upstairs to the Pink Room. It felt even creepier in there in the dark, even with the flashlights. The rain scratching at the windows didn't help; it reminded Jen of the terrifying dream she'd had and made her feel like the storm was trying to get inside.

She set her flashlight down, took the music box from the top of the dresser, and turned the knob on the back of the box.

"I hope this works," she said as she lifted the lid.

"My Bonnie Lies over the Ocean" began to play, the tinkling of the music box filling the room. Maddie and Joe stood on either side of Jen, shining their flashlights around. A Nix slinked into the room and jumped onto the bed, its eyes glinting. The tune ended and began to play again.

"Is she going to come?" Maddie asked.

"I hope so," said Jen.

Someone was humming the song that the music box was playing. Jen, thinking it was Pearl, looked around. Then she realized there was a human source. "Joe!" she said.

"Sorry," Joe said. "I hum when I'm nervous."

They stood, no one talking, as the music box played on. Then Jen heard the humming again.

"That isn't me," Joe said before she could tell him to be quiet.

"My daddy is over the sea," a faint voice sang in time with the music box.

"It's Pearl!" Jen whispered.

"My daddy is over the ocean," Pearl sang, her voice stronger now. "Please bring back my daddy to me."

Maddie gasped. Jen looked up and saw Pearl's reflection in the mirror above the dresser. The three friends turned around. The ghost of Pearl Pratchett stood behind them, in front of her own portrait. She carried the doll head in one hand.

"Hi, Pearl," Jen said. "Thanks for coming." She felt weird, but talking to ghosts was kind of becoming a normal thing for her, so she tried not to think about the fact that Pearl was dead. "We found your doll," she told the spirit.

Maddie, who had carried the doll upstairs, held it out to Pearl. The ghost looked at it for a moment, then reached out. When her fingertips touched Maddie's, Maddie inhaled sharply. "She's cold," she said softly.

The doll body in Maddie's hands began to fade, until it

took on the same foggy appearance that Pearl's ghost had. Maddie let go and stepped back as Pearl fitted the doll head to the body and it became whole again.

"Thank you," Pearl said, holding the doll to her chest.

"There's something else," Jen said. She held up the key that she'd been carrying in her pocket. "Do you know what this goes to?"

Pearl held out her hand. Jen laid the key on her palm, watching as it turned silvery too. Pearl peered at the key, then nodded. "It opens Daddy's chest," she said.

"Great," Joe said. "And where is this chest?"

"In his room," said Pearl.

"And where is *that*?" asked Maddie.

Pearl didn't answer. She was busy hugging her doll and singing to it. And she was fading away.

"Wait!" Jen cried out. "We need to know where his room is!"

"And we need the key!" Maddie added.

Pearl dropped the key. As it fell from her hand it became

solid again, landing on the carpet. Jen reached down and picked it up. When she stood back up, Pearl was gone.

"Great," Maddie said. "Now what?"

"Well, at least we know what the key opens," Joe said. "We just have to find this chest."

"There are a lot of chests in this house," said Jen. She was thinking about all the ones Aunt Liv kept materials for her dolls in. "It could be any of them. Plus, any chest belonging to Captain Pratchett probably isn't even in the house anymore."

"Right," Maddie agreed. "It could have been moved or sold or taken. Like Pearl's doll. That chest could be anywhere by now. We don't even know what it looks like."

"Actually," Jen said, "we might. Come with me."

She picked up her flashlight and made her way back to the first floor, where she went to the portrait of William Pratchett that was painted above the fireplace. She shined her light on it. "See how he's got his hand on the chest?" she said. "I bet that's the one the key goes to."

"Have you seen one in the house like it?" Maddie asked.

"No," Jen said. "But I also haven't been looking for one."

Joe, who was peering closely at the portrait, reached up and touched it.

"What are you doing?" Maddie said.

Joe was rubbing a finger over part of the portrait. "There's a hole here," he said. "In the wood. And it's right where the keyhole on the trunk is." He turned to Jen. "Can I see the key?"

Jen handed him the key. Joe took it and pressed the end of it against the wall. The key slipped inside. He turned it and there was a clicking sound. Then a panel in the wall beside the fireplace sprang open on invisible hinges.

"It's a smuggler's hole!" Maddie said excitedly. "They built them into old houses as places to hide things."

Jen shined her flashlight into the newly revealed opening. Inside was a small space that wasn't large enough to be called a room, but big enough to hold something like a chest. And sitting on the floor was the very chest in the portrait above the fireplace.

Joe removed the key from the hole in the portrait and handed it to Jen. "See if it fits," he said.

Jen's hand shook as she inserted the key into the lock on the chest. She held her breath as she turned it. There was another click, and the lid popped up a little bit. Jen lifted it the rest of the way. Maddie and Joe pressed in close, all three of them looking inside.

The chest was filled with gold coins. Jen took one out and looked at it. Joe snatched up another one and bit it.

"What?" he said when Jen and Maddie looked at him. "You're supposed to do that to see if they're real. I saw it in a movie."

"I think they *are* real," Maddie said. "And there are a *lot* of them."

Jen didn't know what to say. If the coins in the chest were real, she imagined they were worth more than she could even think about. "This is enough to pay the mortgage on Pratchett House!" she said.

"And then some," said Maddie. She laughed. "Jen, your aunt is rich now!"

Jen started to laugh too. But her laughter was cut short when someone turned on a light behind her. She spun around. But the light wasn't coming from any flashlight. It was coming from the figure of a man. He stood in the living room, looking sternly at the three friends who were standing in front of him with gold coins in their hands.

"Captain Pratchett," Jen said. He looked exactly like he did in his portrait.

"Aye," the ghost of William Pratchett said, sounding angry. "What are you doing in my house?"

"We're—" Jen began.

"Stealing my treasure!" Captain Pratchett bellowed.

The light around him changed color, turning the same greenish yellow Jenn had seen before when Pearl appeared to her. It looked like an angry, churning sea. At the same time, the ghost of William Pratchett raised his hands and advanced toward them.

"I don't suppose you have that bottle of Edith's ghost repellant on you?" Joe whispered to Jen.

The ghost drew nearer. Just as the light around him looked stormy, now he did too. His hair blew wildly around his face, and his clothes seemed to be wet. Water dripped from them, and the scent of the ocean was strong. When Jen looked at his face, his eyes had turned pale and cloudy.

He's become the drowned version of himself, she thought.

The captain opened his mouth, and an awful gurgling sound poured out.

"Father!"

A second light flared as the ghost of Pearl Pratchett appeared beside her father. Captain Pratchett turned and looked at her. Pearl held up her doll. "They're not stealing your treasure," she said. "They returned my doll to me."

The light around William Pratchett turned from stormy to clear as moonlight, and he transformed again, until once more he looked like he did in his portrait. "My precious Pearl," he said, holding out his arms.

Pearl stepped into her father's embrace. They held each other for a long time. Then Captain Pratchett turned to look at Joe, Maddie, and Jen. "You have my thanks," he said. "And my treasure." He took Pearl's hand. "But I have the greatest treasure of all."

The light around Pearl and William grew more intense. Jen shielded her eyes from it. Then it went out, and when she looked again, the ghosts were gone.

"Do you hear that?" Joe said.

"Hear what?" said Jen.

"The storm," said Joe. "It's stopped."

The three friends went onto the porch. Sure enough, the day was calm. Even the clouds had moved away. The sky overhead was blue and bright.

"We did it," Maddie said. "We really did it."

"And nobody is going to believe it," said Jen. "What are we going to tell everyone?"

"You'd better think of something fast," Joe told her. "Because here comes your aunt. And the Toms. And my uncle and Rita."

Sure enough, all those people were walking up the road toward Pratchett House. When they reached the porch, Aunt Liv said, "Are you all right?"

Jen nodded. "We're fine," she said. "And have we got a story for you."

THREE DAYS LATER

"Well, that settles it," Aunt Liv said. She held up a folded-up piece of paper. "The chest belonging to Captain William Pratchett officially belongs to me."

The small group gathered at Soco's cheered.

"You mean you get to keep all the money?" Jen said.

"Well, I *could* keep it all," Liv said. "But I'm not going to."

"What do you mean?" said Maddie.

"I feel like the chest belongs to Big Rock Island," Liv said. "So, I'm going to use the money to help the people who live here. I'll pay off the mortgage on Pratchett House, along with any other mortgages people on the island have. Then some of the money will be used to make improvements on

215

the island and some will go into a trust to pay for college or trade school educations for any resident who wants to go."

"Wow," Joe said. "I wish I still lived on the island."

"You'll always be an islander," Aunt Liv said. "And eligible for a scholarship."

"There's enough to do all that?" Jen asked.

Her aunt nodded. "With some left over," she said.

"All thanks to Pearl and William Pratchett," Jen said.

"I bet you never thought your stay on Big Rock would be this exciting," Aunt Liv said.

"And I've only been here a week," Jen said. "I wonder what else will happen."

"The Big Rock Grand Prix is coming up," Maddie reminded her. "It's not *quite* as exciting as looking for ghost treasure, but I'm looking forward to winning again this year."

"We'll see about that," Jen told her, laughing. "Joe and I might surprise you."

A lot had happened in the three days since Jen and her friends found the treasure hidden in Pratchett House.

They'd told Aunt Liv and the others about Chester McKiser's plan, and about finding the key inside Pearl Pratchett's doll and putting the clues together. They left out the part about the ghosts helping them, and everyone was so excited about the treasure that no one asked too many questions.

As for Chester, the Toms found him swimming out to sea while they were checking on their lobster traps after the storm. They picked him up in their boat and brought him in. He was rambling about sirens and hearing them calling to him, so they took him over to the mainland, where he was admitted to a hospital for observation. Aunt Olivia told the authorities about what he'd done, and it looked like he wouldn't be causing any more trouble on Big Rock Island.

Everyone hung out, celebrating, until it was dark and time to head home. Jen said good night to her friends, then she and Aunt Liv started the walk home. When they came to the fork in the road, Jen said, "Is it okay if I go look at the lighthouse for a little while?"

"Sure," Liv said. "Just be careful. I'll see you at home."

Home. Jen liked how the word sounded. Big Rock Island wasn't her home in the same way it was for Aunt Liv, Maddie, and the others. She was only there for the summer. Still, she knew the island was a kind of home for her now too. And that felt good.

She walked to the lighthouse. Standing outside it, she thought about everything that had happened, not only a few nights earlier but two hundred years ago. She was happy that Pearl and William Pratchett seemed to have found a happy ending to their story. But she felt bad for Arthur Crunk. He'd helped her and Joe and Maddie a lot.

She looked up at the lighthouse tower. She wondered what would become of the place now. She hoped Aunt Liv would be able to buy it somehow and turn it into a place where people could come and learn about its history.

As she looked up at the windowed room at the top of the tower, a light came on. It extended out in a beam that touched the surface of the sea. Jen knew from being up there that the light didn't work anymore, so she had no idea how this was possible. But it was on. Then she realized that the light wasn't quite the same as regular light. It was more silvery.

Ghostly, she thought.

Then a shadow appeared against the windows. Someone was up there. The figure stepped into the light, and for a moment Jen saw a man's face. It was Arthur Crunk. He looked down at Jen, then lifted his hand and waved.

Jen waved back.

Then she turned around and started to walk home.

ANOTHER CHILLING TALE!

At first, twin sisters Ava and Cassie are excited to move into a ramshackle old mansion in a new town. But any romantic ideas they had are quickly dashed. The house is dirty, dusty, and falling apart. Worse, it's infamous around town as "that creepy old haunted house."

When the sisters remove some wallpaper in the bedroom, they find childlike drawings of a screaming girl. Then Cassie starts acting oddly. Ava can't put her finger on it, but she's just not quite herself. And if Cassie's not herself, then who is she becoming?

ABOUT THE AUTHOR

Mike Ford is the author of numerous spooky books, including titles in the Eerie, Indiana; Spinetinglers; and Frightville series. He started writing about haunted things after growing up in a house full of ghosts who wanted him to tell them bedtime stories.